THE CAPO'S MISTRESS

Richard Harris

Durban House

Copyright © 2007, Richard Harris

All rights reserved. No part of this book may be used or reproduced in any manner whatsoever without the written permission of the Publisher.

Printed in the United States of America.

For information address:
Durban House Publishing Company, Inc.
7502 Greenville Avenue, Suite 500, Dallas, Texas 75231

Library of Congress Cataloging-in-Publication Data

Harris, Richard, 1927 -

The Capo's Mistress / Richard Harris

Library of Congress Control Number: 2005935730

p. cm.

ISBN 1-930754-82-5
First Edition

10 9 8 7 6 5 4 3 2 1

Visit our Web site at
http://www.durbanhouse.com

This book is dedicated to my wife, Maggi, the love of my life.

The characters in this novel are fictional. Any similarity to real persons, living or dead, is purely coincidental.

Acknowledgements

Thanks to John Lewis for his faith in this project,

my editor, Robert Middlemiss, for his patience, professionalism and Navy stories,

Jennifer Adkins for her careful reading of the manuscript,

and to my wife, Maggi, and my children, Margaret, Dick, Anne, John, Will and Joe, for their support and encouragement.

THE CAPO'S MISTRESS

chapter one

I left Henry's Lake early Saturday morning on my way to Helena, then back to L.A. The trip had been a bust. I don't know what I was looking for but I didn't find it at Five's place. He was my first partner on the L.A.P.D. when I got out of the Academy. I was nineteen and they assigned me to an old timer to learn the ropes. His name was Tom Faris and he had been on the force eight years. Five was a nickname he got later. I looked at him as my mentor but he was a bad teacher for someone just out of the Academy. Five had been on the take for years. Not big stuff like drug deals but not doughnuts either.

He looked the other way for street pushers and pimps. I didn't catch on at first but it was pretty easy to figure out. After a while he knew I knew and he offered to cut me in. In those days the lowest scum on earth was a cop who turned in his partner, I mean among cops, so I kind of went along with it and took my share of the money and the women. I like to think that's what caused me to start drinking and maybe it did, then again maybe I'm just looking for an excuse. I know now that I was becoming more and more disillusioned. I joined the force to make a difference but I was getting like Five. When we caught a bad guy and had him alone Five would really work him over before calling for backup. This was before we had to worry about video cameras. When we got to the station the report would say that the guy resisted arrest and had to be subdued. I would sign it and hate myself for doing it. After awhile I felt like wailing on someone myself and I would join in with Five on some poor son of a bitch.

I usually like to drive alone. The radio is off, the cell phone is off, the windows are rolled up and I let my thoughts keep me company. But today I was beating myself up. When I got to Five's place I hadn't had a drink for seven years, eight months and sixteen days. Now it's been about 5 hours and I need another drink bad. I'm going to Helena to find an A.A. meeting before I start the long drive back to L.A.

Five called me when he heard I had retired and invited me up to take a look at Idaho. When I got there he had some friends over to meet me, ex-cops and mostly living alone, like me. Five never married and my wife left me over the drinking and gambling and women. I couldn't blame her. Thank God we didn't have any kids.

As soon as they all got to Five's house the drinking started. I told Five I didn't drink anymore and asked for a soda. He started in on me and so did the others. I should have walked out right there but I didn't. Instead I got loaded, started playing poker and lost $200 I couldn't afford to lose.

I realize now that I stopped drinking when Five retired and moved to Idaho. After I was sober awhile I tried to look up my wife to see if we could get back together. I found out she had remarried so I left well enough alone.

I guess I went back to see Five because I was lonely and didn't know what to do with myself. As long as I was on the force my life had some meaning, there was something that I had to do every day. I griped about it and so did everyone else, but my life such as it was had a structure. Now that's gone. I get up every day and wonder how I'm going to get through it without a drink.

Five and his buddies have the same problem. They've got each other and that's about it. All they talked about was guns and hunting and dogs. Five always was a crack shot. He spent a lot of time on the firing range because he didn't have anything else to do. That's how he got his nickname.

We were on duty and spotted this kid boosting a radio out of a car. When we grabbed him you could tell he was scared but he had a lot of mouth and called us a couple of motherfuckers. That pissed Five off and he pulled his gun out and pointed it at the kid. I thought he was just screwing around, and he probably was, but the kid gave him the finger and Five shot it off. The kid was standing right behind it and the bullet went through his right eye. Now we had a dead kid on our hands.

Five pulled out a throw down piece and put it in the kid's hand, then he called for backup. We wrote up the report that the kid drew down on us and Five shot him, but it turned out that the shot-off finger was on his right hand and the kid was right-handed, so how did one bullet take off his right middle finger while the kid was holding the gun and enter the brain through his right eye? Charges were brought and the review board bought our story that the bullet hit the kid's finger and gun and ricocheted into the eye socket.

The D.A. filed on it because of the bad press he was receiving for doing nothing, but the jury verdict mirrored the findings of the review board and we thought we were home free. Then the kid's mother and father brought a civil action against the city and us and they got a hell of a good lawyer to do it. Their expert witnesses testified it was impossible for the bullet to have ricocheted into the eye socket because the middle finger of the boy would have been below the trigger guard, if he was holding the gun, and the bullet would have been deflected downward, not upward. The jury verdict was five million dollars. We started calling Tom the Five Million Dollar Man and that's how he got his nickname. He grew to love it.

I have to admit the country is every bit as beautiful as Five and his buddies told me. I just crossed into Montana from Idaho and I'm driving alongside the Madison River, according to the map. It's a real river, which always amazes someone like me who was born and raised in L.A. By that I mean that the river looks to be about 75 feet wide and it's full of fast running water in late September. In L.A. everything is dry by now and even in the spring you never see anything that looks like this. The water is always in concrete-lined flood control channels being escorted out to sea by the cement.

Every now and then I pass a fisherman on the bank or in waders in the river and the trees are starting to turn gold. There's a chill in the air, although the sun is shining down brightly, and I'm sure God invented football to go along with this weather. This would be a great place to live if Five hadn't found it first but I don't want to be within a thousand miles of him. I want to get sober and stay sober and find something to do with the rest of my life. A job of some kind but one I can be proud of, not just flipping hamburgers or something like that. I'm 49 years old and I'm lost.

I stopped beating myself up and drove along the Madison River, not thinking, just taking in the scenery. It was certainly worth the trouble. I was wondering how far I had to be away from Five to live here and not see him anymore when the right front end of my clunker dropped onto the pavement at 70 miles an hour. No warning like you get from the noise of a tire blowing, just the sound of metal grinding on the pavement and the sight of sparks flying up from the roadway. The car lurched to the right and put me almost broadside to the highway. I could feel it start to roll and it took the best corrective action in the manual to keep from going over. I finally came to a stop with the car at a 90-degree angle to the highway and got out to see what had happened. The right front wheel was off and about thirty yards behind. The hub had dug into the asphalt and left a big ugly scar for about the same distance. I was lucky to be alive.

It was time for the cell phone. I called the Auto Club of Southern California and tried to explain why I was calling from Montana and where I was. I told them I had left from Henry's Lake, the number of the highway, for about how long I had been driving, and that I was alongside the Madison River. They told me they would have a tow truck come get me. I retrieved the front wheel and tire and got back in the car to sit and wait. I didn't have a book to read so I just sat there and watched the river.

I had seen only a few cars all morning and the highway was empty and stayed that way for the next half hour, then a pickup truck came along and I told the guy help was on its way. He drove off, promising to report my location to the sheriff when he got to town. He didn't say where town was and I forgot to ask. Another 20 minutes went by before the tow truck arrived. The driver kneeled down to look at the front end without saying anything, then stood up and said, "Looks like your front wheel bearing gave out. I'll tow you to a garage in Virginia City."

"No way," I said, "that's over 500 miles from here. I'm not going to pay for your next truck."

"More like five miles, but suit yourself," he said.

He started to get in his truck without hooking me up.

"What do you mean, five miles?"

He looked me up and down. "I see by your plates you're

from California. I hope you're not planning to move here. We've got enough of your kind already."

Right then and there I changed my mind about settling down here.

"I can't get out of here fast enough," I replied, "just get me to a garage so I can get started."

I climbed into the passenger seat and saw that the name on the door of the truck was Jeb Breckenridge but he didn't introduce himself, and I sure as hell wasn't going to break the ice, so we drove in silence all the way to the garage in Virginia City. He took my Auto Club card, ran it through his machine, and drove away without saying a word. I didn't say anything either. A couple of soreheads. The guy who owned the garage was another matter. He introduced himself as Sam Culpepper, stuck out his hand to shake mine, and put my car up on the hoist.

"It's the front wheel bearing, all right, and your hub was really chewed up by the road. I'll have to send to Helena for parts."

I didn't like the sound of that "all right." He had to have talked to the tow truck driver.

"How long will that take?" I asked.

"Today's Saturday. They won't be open until Monday and the parts won't get here 'til Tuesday. I'll have you up and running by Wednesday or Thursday."

He said all this with a big smile, as if to say, I've got you now.

"My God, that will be October," I said.

"If you say so," he replied.

I decided to ask for mercy. "Look, can't you do any better then that? I'm almost out of money and I can't afford to stay here that long."

"Won't cost you that much," he replied. "This weekend is the end of the season. Everything shuts down after that. The motels will be so glad to see you that you can name your own price. I'll do my best to get you out of here as quick as I can. You have my word on that."

He gave me that smile again and I looked around the garage. Mine was the only car in it. No wonder he was smiling. It wasn't just the motels that were hurting for business.

"What do you do around here?" I asked in a resigned voice.

"There's great fishing in the river. Do you like to fish?"

I gave him a half-hearted shrug that meant I didn't much care about fishing and he looked at me with real pity.

"City boy, huh?"

"Born and raised in L.A.," I replied.

Now he looked really sorry for me.

"How about horseback riding?" he asked hopefully.

I shook my head from side to side, beginning to feel like a freak.

"What kind of business you in?" he asked.

"I just retired after thirty years on the L.A.P.D."

He brightened perceptibly. "Hunting, I'll bet you like to hunt. How about going after some elk?"

"Look," I replied, "maybe I'll just take a walk around town and find a place to stay."

He looked happy at this.

"Be sure to see Old Town. If you never heard of Virginia City, Montana, you're gonna be surprised. This was a real Wild West town with a real gold rush and saloons and whores and vigilantes. The vigilantes even hung the sheriff."

"Sounds like my kind of place," I said and started for town. "I'll come back to pick up my stuff after I find a motel."

"There's even a Boot Hill and a Railroad Museum," he called after me.

He was right about the season being over. The merchants looked hopefully out at me as I passed the few stores that were still open for business. I found Old Town without any difficulty and walked down the middle of the main street and there was not another tourist in sight. It felt like Tombstone at high noon with all the citizens hiding in their stores until the gunfight was over. I took a self-guided tour, going from store to store and sign to sign. It really was pretty interesting, especially because I had never heard of Virginia City, Montana, until a few hours ago.

Just like my friend in the garage said, there was a gold rush here. I wandered down the street to the store of Kiskadden and Company, where the vigilantes signed their oath, and imagined what the town looked like then. Not so long ago: no automobiles, airplanes, freeways, radio, TV, internet or a million other things, only horses and buggies. It didn't sound bad.

I saw the location of the first building in Virginia City, a bakery, between the Sauerbier Blacksmith Shop and the Bale of Hay Saloon. The saloon in turn connected to the Opera House, which was a thoughtful touch for the opera lovers in town. Across the street were the Green Front Hotel and the railroad depot. A voice behind me said, "Isn't it just like I told you?"

I turned and it was Sam Culpepper from the garage.

"Yeah, it's something to see, all right," I agreed.

Sam looked happy. "I close the garage early on Saturday and I thought I'd come by to tell you your car is in the lot and give you the keys." He handed them to me.

"While I'm here let me tell you some stuff that you don't see on the signs. Did you know that most of the people who came here for the gold rush were from the South? This was right in the middle of the Civil War. Did you know that?"

"No," I said, wondering how long the lecture would last.

"It's true," Sam continued. "There's a monument to the Confederacy in Helena, and this town was first named Varina, after the wife of Jeff Davis, the President of the Confederate

States. President Lincoln couldn't let all the gold go to the Confederacy, what with this being Union territory and all, so he brought in settlers from the North to help hold the gold for the Union. That's how the vigilantes got started."

"How's that?" I asked in spite of myself.

"Well," Sam replied, "most people believe that the Northerners formed the vigilantes and hung Southerners, not just crooks, to keep the gold for the Union. They even hung the sheriff, like I said. Others say that the vigilantes were necessary to restore law and order and that the sheriff was the secret leader of the robbers that were hijacking the gold shipments. Nobody really knows.

"Like I said, Montana was full of Confederate sympathizers during the Civil War, and if gold hadn't of been discovered there wouldn't have been any vigilantes. But in 1863 gold was discovered, and a lot of it, and whichever side got the gold would probably win the Civil War because it would make their paper money worth something. During the war it took a wheelbarrow full of Confederate money to buy a loaf of bread, but the gold from Virginia City saved the Union greenback."

Sam stopped talking and I gave him a little hand of applause. The guy knew his stuff, or at least it seemed to me he did. He could have been making it all up but I didn't think so. This was history that wasn't taught in school, the story behind the story, like the guy on the radio says.

"Thanks for your trouble, Sam," I said, "that helps me understand what went on here. I'm going to keep looking around for a while."

He took the hint. "Be sure to see the hotel and the railroad depot," he said. "The Railroad Museum closes tomorrow for the season."

"I will," I said and started to cross the street.

I looked at the Green Front Hotel and imagined I was a passenger arriving by train in the 1860s. I walked over to the railroad depot, turned around, and pretended I was leaving the depot and heading for the Green Front. It was eerie. There was no one around to break the spell, and I was back in the Wild West arriving to make my fortune panning for gold.

"Just get off the train, Mister?" a laughing feminine voice called out from behind me.

I spun around, feeling my cheeks turn red, so close was the guess to what I was actually imagining, but there was no one there. I looked around, confused.

"Here I am," the voice said. It was in the ticket booth of the Railroad Museum and asked, "Would you like to buy a ticket?"

I walked over to the booth, out of the bright sunlight, and saw her for the first time. She was about 35 and dressed in a big, floppy sweater and jeans because of the chill in the air. She wore her hair tucked into an engineer's cap, with a few wisps of blonde escaping, and no make-up, but she couldn't hide the fact that she was gorgeous, which made my embarrassment all the more acute. She took pity on me.

"I see people do that all the time," she said, "especially when they think no one is around. It's a common fantasy, I guess, going back in time. I do it myself."

Eight years ago I would have had no chance with her. I was a drunk and weighed 240 pounds. My stomach rolled over the top of my belt and my uniform looked like it was about to burst. My face was bigger than Teddy Kennedy's. When I joined the force I was 6 feet tall and weighed 175 pounds, so you can get some idea of the terrible shape I was in.

After I stopped drinking I got into running and martial arts to take my mind off the booze. My goal was to get good enough to join the L.A.P.D. running team, and I did. It's a team that runs from L.A. to Las Vegas and once ran across the country, each member running a fixed number of miles from a mother van carrying the whole team. The fat melted away until I hit 185 pounds and by the time I retired I was a black belt in karate and teaching martial arts at the Academy. Why not? After I gave up the booze there was nothing else to do. Anyway, I no longer considered myself a slob and checked to see if she wore a wedding ring. She didn't. I also let her see that I was checking so she'd know I was interested.

She smiled and asked again, "Would you like to buy a ticket?"

The sign said five bucks and I didn't have five bucks to spend to see some old trains, but I needed a reason to hang around. I pulled out my credit card.

"Okay," I said.

She smiled again and said she would have to have some identification so I pulled out my copper-stopper, which is where I keep my driver's license. A copper-stopper, in case you don't know, is a leather case for your driver's license on one side and your police badge on the other. The idea is to afford a graceful way to let the cop who has just stopped you for speeding know that you are a brother officer, whether retired or not. It also helps in situations like this.

She looked at me, no longer smiling. "Are you a policeman?" she asked.

I laughed and tried my best to look charming.

"Hey, retired from the L.A.P.D. Don't hold it against me."

She relaxed and smiled again.

"You look too young to be retired," she said.

"Thank you, young lady," I said, which made her laugh for the first time.

"You're the first visitor today, believe it or not, so take a look around on the house. No charge for police officers, even retired ones. We close in about an hour."

I thanked her and pushed my way through the turnstile. The museum held all kind of trains, real ones, full size. There were old ones dating back to the days when passengers shot buffalo from the train windows for sport, trains from the golden age of railroading with Pullman cars and dining cars and observation decks, millionaires' private cars in all their splendor, and engines of every description to pull the cars over mountains and across the country. A railroad buff could spend days in here. It took me half an hour because I wanted to get back before closing with lots of time left to get to know the girl in the booth. I figured if I was going to spend five days here it would help to have some company. She smiled when I came back out.

"That didn't take long," she said. "Don't you like trains?"

"It made me kind of sad, to tell you the truth. It reminded me of an elephants' graveyard."

She started. "That's so strange. I often have that thought. All these old trains once so vital to the country have been brought here to this one place to rot in the sun and the snow. It is sad. I've never said it out loud before." She looked like she might cry.

"Hey," I said, "I didn't mean to bring you down. Just the opposite."

I stuck out my hand. "My name's Mike Driscoll."

She took it and said, "I'm Mary Carter."

chapter two

    I'm not a lady-killer by any means but I do love women. I like the way they look, the way they smell, the way they walk, the way they can knock you dead with one glance, how graceful they are, the way they laugh and everything about them. I love to make love to them over and over until we both are exhausted. I love to watch them go by and pretend we have just made love. Sometimes they glare at me because they have read my mind and sometimes they smile for the same reason. They are totally unpredictable, which makes me love them more. The problem is that you can't be with all of them at once, only one at a time, and when you are with one, even a beautiful one, you still can't help watching the others go by. There was no one else to watch now, however, and I was alone with Mary Carter, who was very beautiful indeed. I searched for something else to say. She came to the rescue.

    "It's pretty late in the year to visit Virginia City," she said. "We close the museum tomorrow for the season and I'll be out of a job."

"I'm an involuntary visitor," I explained, and went through my tale of woe. I told her I would be here until next Wednesday or Thursday and asked, "Can you recommend someplace to stay that's cheap but clean? I wasn't expecting a car repair bill and it's going to be a big one, I can tell by the gleam in the garage owner's eyes. Mine is the only car in the place and it's going to be a long winter."

She looked me up and down and asked with a smile, "Can you behave yourself?"

I didn't know what was coming and said, "Yes, ma'am, I've been doing that for the last thirty years and it's too late to change now."

"Look," she said, "I wouldn't normally suggest this, but I'm out of a job after tomorrow and the rent's due next week. I have one of those sofas that pull out into a bed. If you don't mind sleeping on that I'll throw in breakfast every morning for $25 a night."

I tried not to look like the cat that ate the canary as I said "yes." The possibilities were endless.

"Where are your things?" she asked.

I told her that I had to get them out of my car in the garage and she handed me a key.

"The address is 27 Jackson Street. Go get your bags and I'll meet you there after I close up. If you want to pick up a couple of steaks and a bottle of wine along the way, I'll cook dinner for us."

The damn cat-and-canary smile was all over my face, I couldn't control it. I put the key in my pocket and said, "Sounds great. See you there."

I got my stuff from the car, just a duffel bag really, and walked into town. It wasn't much bigger than Old Town and I had no trouble finding Jackson Street. I dropped the duffel bag on the porch of number 27, then started to look for a market. I suddenly noticed I was smiling as I walked along the street and that I felt great. Just this morning I was beating myself up for drinking and gambling and losing $200, then the car broke down and I got even lower. Now I'm on top of the world. If the car hadn't given out on me I would have flashed right by this little burg. The hippies call it karma, others call it fate and some say that's the way the ball bounces, but things were definitely looking up for me. I found a market and picked out two great looking steaks. The old credit card was going to take a beating this week but I didn't worry about it. When I got home there were sure to be two or three applications for credit cards in the mail and I'd just shift my debts to a new bank. I was helping the economy, according to our President, and I was going to be a real patriot this week.

I picked out a nice bottle of wine. If Mary Carter wanted wine with her dinner she was going to have it. I recalled the verse, "Candy is dandy but liquor is quicker," tossed in another bottle, then stopped short. I certainly didn't want to get drunk. I could tell her I'm a recovering alcoholic, that's the phrase we use, but I rejected the idea right away. It was way too early to bring up that subject. When I was on the force and a drunk the only women who would go out with me were the prostitutes on my beat, and they did because their pimp told them they had to. Women do not want to be stuck with a drunk, even a happy one.

After a couple of drinks I become the life of the party; after a few more my memory shuts down but I'm still able to get around, so they tell me; and after a few more I pass out cold and wake up in the morning with a terrible hangover. When I swore off the booze I became socially eligible again even though I was still a 240-pound slob. I started to get invited to dinner by married couples and there would be a single woman who had also been invited, which was embarrassing for both of us: me because I was still a fat slob and her because it was obvious our hosts thought this was the best she could do.

My point is that being an alcoholic, even a recovering one, is not something to bring up on a first date, which is the way I thought of tonight's dinner. I decided I would drink along with her but try to keep it under control, two or three glasses of wine at the most while keeping her glass full. After a while she wouldn't notice or care that I wasn't keeping up with her. I put another bottle of wine in the cart, white for before dinner, and picked up some peanuts to go along with it.

When I got back to the house she was there and the lights were on. I knocked rather than use the key and she opened the door. She had gotten rid of the baggy sweater and jeans, replaced with what I think is called a hostess gown, all in green, which matched two eyes the color of emeralds. The engineer's cap was gone and her blonde hair spilled onto the shoulders of the green gown.

"Hi," she said, "did you find the market?"

I was dumbstruck. I tried to say something and it wouldn't come out. I pretended to clear my throat.

"Yeah," I said, "do you feel like a meal?"

Only it came out sounding more like "mule" than "meal." Brilliant, I thought, absolutely brilliant, I asked her if she felt like a mule. She was no dummy and knew that she had just turned me into a schoolboy again. Women can do that, which is one of the reasons I love them. They're mysterious and magical and you never know what they will do next, like the spell she had just cast on me when she opened the door. Men are their natural prey and at their mercy. I remembered a newspaper story I had read awhile back about a crime ring in Japan which had used women to ensnare rich married men and then blackmail them. One of the women had said, "Men are such imbeciles." It was true, which caused me to wonder as a cop, retired or not, what this beautiful woman saw in me and why she was stuck in a burg like this selling tickets at a side show to Old Town.

She gave me a sweet smile, took the grocery bag from me and said, "I'm starved. Come in and make yourself comfortable while I fix dinner."

I picked up my duffel bag from the porch and went inside. It was a tiny wood frame house at least a hundred years old. The front door opened into what passed for a living room, with a little fireplace, and to my left was a dining area and kitchen. The hall led to a bath and bedroom and that was it. She had a CD on playing soft music, which I took as a good sign, and put my duffel bag down next to the sofa, the only one in the living room, and therefore my bed at $25 a night, with breakfast thrown in, plus a chance at what I was hoping for. It was the bargain of the century. I walked into the kitchen, where she was unloading the grocery bag and just pulling out the third bottle of wine.

"I hope this is for the week," she laughed.

"I bought a bottle of white and some peanuts to have before dinner. Can I light a fire?"

She shivered and said, "Oh, that sounds so warm and cozy. It was cold walking home. Next month it will start to snow, everyone says."

That gave me an opening and I asked, "How long have you lived here?"

"Only since March," she replied. "I stopped here for gas and I needed a job. Everything was just opening up for the tourist season and I went to work at the Railroad Museum. Now everything's closing for the winter and I don't want to be here then, so I'll have to move on."

"Let me start that fire and open the wine and we can discuss your future," I said.

I've found it's pretty easy to talk to women, particularly beautiful women, if you aren't blind-sided by their beauty, which is what happened to me at the front door. Once you get them in a conversation, ask them to tell you about themselves and they open right up, because this is their favorite subject. One of the first things I learned as a cop is that people like to talk about themselves and can hardly wait for you to stop talking so they can grab the floor again, and that if you can shut up yourself and just listen the suspect will probably hang himself or herself. This applies particularly to beautiful women because they're so stuck on themselves. I built the fire like a Boy Scout, which I once was, crossing the logs carefully so they would get plenty of air, then lit it and opened the wine and the peanuts and got a couple of glasses while the fire was getting started. When it was roaring I called her to come out of the kitchen and she did, again momentarily stunning me when the fire reflected from those emerald eyes.

"Oh, how beautiful," she said.

"You are," I replied, and she beamed at me and sat on the sofa facing the fire.

I poured us both a glass of wine, making mine smaller than hers, and sat down beside her. I held my glass up to her and she touched it with hers and took a sip of wine.

"Now tell me about yourself, Mary Carter, I want to know all about you," I said.

She snuggled down in the sofa.

"Well, there's not much to tell." But she didn't mean it.

"I was born in Bisbee, Arizona, and did the usual things as a kid, soccer, Girl Scouts, high school cheerleader and high school plays. I wanted to be an actress and after high school I went to Hollywood instead of college, which broke my parents' hearts. Hollywood was hard, as you probably know. The casting couch system is alive and well, only now it's the agents and actors who promise you a break instead of the producers. I didn't want to play that game, so I left and went to Las Vegas and got a job as a chorus girl at the Tropicana, where I thought I would be discovered, but I never got a chance to show anyone that I had any talent except for large breasts. I was a topless show girl who stood on top of a pillar with my back to the audience and turned around on cue, then danced in the chorus line when the stage show started. That went on for five years, believe it or not, before I came to my senses and realized I was never going to do anything else until I got too old to be in the chorus line and my breasts started to sag. I went to classes and became a blackjack dealer at Treasure Island, where they liked me because I was a pretty good dealer and my looks kept my table full of guys trying to pick me up. It was a steady job and I got good tips and didn't have to expose myself every night to a bunch of drunks, and that's what I did until I came here."

She stopped for breath and took a big gulp of wine. I had probably been one of those drunks, I thought ruefully, and asked the obvious question. "Why did you leave?"

"That's a long story," she said. "I think I'll save that for another time and enjoy the wine and the fire and the company."

She snuggled down more in the sofa and I thought she moved closer to me.

I wondered if I should say, "Poor kid," and put my arm around her, which may have been what she wanted, but I decided it was too big a chance to take this early. I took a little sip of wine and held up my glass again and said, "Here's to karma," trying to sound like something I wasn't. She touched my glass and waited for more.

"Just think," I said. "If my car hadn't broken down and you hadn't stopped for gas neither one of us would be here and we would never have met. Before today I thought the only Virginia City was in Nevada."

"Me, too," she said, "until I pulled into the gas station."

She sat silently, pondering the mysteries and meaning of this. I changed my mind and put my arm around her. Big mistake, I broke the spell.

"I've got to get dinner ready," she said, and went into the kitchen.

The fire flickered on the glasses on the table at dinner. A wind had come up and it had started to rain outside, but we were cozy and warm and the first bottle of red was almost gone although there was still plenty of steak on our plates. I had limited myself to two glasses of red plus about half a glass of white in the other room, which took a lot of effort, and her glass was almost empty again.

"This is delicious," I said for the third time. The steak was grilled just the way I had asked and she served it with a baked potato with sour cream and chives and a crisp green salad.

"Save room for dessert," she said. "I didn't have time to bake anything so I picked up something on my way home."

"You're too good to be true," I said and meant it. "Do I have any competition in town?"

It was a dumb question and I wished I had it back the minute I asked it.

Suddenly she looked sad and answered, "No, I dated a few times when I first got here, but one was very jealous and put the other boy in the hospital. He also punched me in the eye. I had quite a shiner for a week or so and decided since I wasn't going to stay here I would just stop dating. I'll be glad to get away from here. It's a small town and he gives me the creeps when I bump into him. Sometimes he hangs around my work and acts very charming. He thinks that I'll forgive him but there's no way. I can still see his face when he hit me. It was horrible."

I felt my temper rising. I wanted to find this guy and show him what getting worked over felt like.

"What's his name?" I asked.

She guessed what I was thinking and took my hand.

"Drop it," she said and smiled again. "Sorry to burden you with my troubles. How about you? Who's waiting for you at home?"

Now it was my turn to answer and I said lamely, "No one.

I was married once but it didn't work out."

She left the answer alone and we looked for a better subject.

"If you don't want to be here for the winter, where are you going to go? L.A., I hope."

"Maybe," she said and paused, then added, "if you coax me."

"Lady, you're going to get a lot of coaxing the next few days. If I do it right maybe you'll come to L.A. with me when my car's ready and you can forget about next month's rent."

"We'll see," she said, and gave me a smile that melted me right down to my socks.

Dessert was little pastries, I think they call them petit fours, served with strong coffee. It was perfect after the steak and wine and I thought about doing this for the rest of my life. It was too bad she didn't want to stay here, right in this little house, with snow outside up to the windows and me bringing in wood for a fire so the house would be warm all night while we snuggled in bed. I said as much to her. I thought it was a good way of planting that notion in her mind so she might like to try it out, and got an enigmatic but kind of dreamy smile in return.

I thought maybe the wine was taking effect but then she stood up and said, "I've got to do the dishes. Tomorrow's a work day for me. My last day." Then she let out a loud, "Whoopee," which took me totally by surprise. The wine was definitely taking effect.

"Let me help," I said.

We carried the plates into the kitchen and she washed while I dried. An oldie was playing on the stereo, nice and slow, and I turned her to me and we started to dance. She put her head on my shoulder and I wished this moment could go on forever, not bed, or making love, just this moment, forever and ever and ever.

The song ended and she looked up at me and said, "That was nice."

I kissed her softly, putting into it all that I was feeling at that moment, and she did the same. The kiss seemed to last forever, which is the way I wanted it, not wanting it to end, and neither did she. At last we broke.

She looked up at me and said, "You don't have to sleep on the sofa tonight."

There was no feeling of triumph in me, no congratulations to myself for all my careful planning, for the wine or for anything else. It was just the opposite. I wished I hadn't bought the wine because maybe that was what had brought about this special moment, so pure to me, and I didn't want it tainted in any way. I kissed her again, the same way, and we hung there, enjoying the closeness of each other, until we could keep our lips together no longer.

She gave me a long slow smile, catlike as if she were purring, and said, "I'll be waiting."

A man always worries about the first time with a woman. After you've been together awhile you get to know her, what she likes and what she doesn't like, how to please her, and what she expects from you. You can have a bad day, or night, and maybe laugh at it, too much liquor, a hard day at work, whatever, you'll do better next time. But the first time has to go well because there's no racing form on you to tell how good you were in your last outing, so the pressure to perform is on you, and you know it. Some of these thoughts went through my mind as I got my pajamas out of the duffel bag in the living room.

"I'll be waiting," she had said, the words I dreamed of since our first meeting, and now I had the jitters, almost like the way you feel when the coach calls your name to go into the game.

Everything will be okay, I told myself, and I was right. I

was so head over heels in love with her that night I could do no wrong. I rolled off her and felt like lighting up two cigarettes, like the guy in the movie, handing one to her and asking, "Was it good for you?"

But then she crawled up on top of me looking for more and there was none. I was like a fighter I used to watch at the Olympic in L.A., a young Irish kid who would bless himself when the bell rang for the first round and run from his corner throwing punches from all angles at his opponent. Sometimes he knocked the other kid out but if that didn't happen there was nothing left for the second round. He had punched himself out. I was in a ten rounder, at least, and I was hanging on for my life. It was humiliating, or at least ironic, that what I had dreamed of all day was on top of me and my poor spent gladiator, moving up and down in sexual frenzy, and I couldn't do anything about it. She didn't seem to care, which was a blessing. She would rest awhile, and I would think she was finished, but then she would moan and start up again. I tried to count the number, got up to at least eight, and longed to get back into the game, but my side had retired from the field. I cursed the gladiator under my breath for fleeing the battle, the dirty little coward. She finally seemed to be satisfied but every now and then she would shudder and move up and down briefly on her cowardly opponent, rubbing in the complete and total victory she had achieved over him. Sometimes her shudders would start her off again and I would increase the count by one, sometimes not. This was her way of cooling down, like walking a thoroughbred racehorse, until she fell asleep, still on top of me.

The alarm went off like a bomb. She gave me a kiss on the cheek while I was still trying to figure out where I was and headed for the bathroom, calling over her shoulder, "I've got to get to work. Stay in bed while I shower and get breakfast. I'll call you when it's ready."

Where I was and the evening before came back to me in Technicolor and I could still hear rain on the shingle roof. It was the kind of day to stay in bed, keep warm and enjoy one another, and I cursed her damn job and that she wasn't in bed here beside me instead of in the shower. She came back into the room wrapped in a towel and her blonde hair was wet and stringy from the shower and sticking to her face and neck. She looked achingly lovely and I asked her to call in sick and come back to bed with me or at least be late for work. She laughed and dropped the towel, slowly put on her bra and panties, and asked sweetly, "Will you miss me while I'm gone?"

I let her see that the dirty little coward was up and active, strutting as if the humiliation of the night before had never occurred, and said, "What do you think?"

She gave the coward a squeeze, pulled on her jeans and floppy sweater, and walked out of the room barefoot, saying as she left, "Now I've got to wash my hands again before I fix breakfast."

I showered and shaved and joined her at the table. She was already eating and I said, "There's no hurry. It's pouring out. You won't have a customer all day."

"I know that," she replied, "but the owner shows up every morning, rain or shine, to make sure I open up on time. He docks me if I'm late and I need the money."

"What does he pay you?" I asked.

"Ten dollars an hour," she replied glumly. "On Sunday we're open from ten to four so that's sixty bucks. You can see why I took in a boarder."

I couldn't understand why she had left Vegas and a job as a dealer, which probably paid at least fifty to seventy-five thousand a year, including tips, to come here. I was thinking like a cop and something didn't add up. She guessed my thoughts and said softly, "I had to leave my last job. That's why I'm here. That's what you were wondering, isn't it?"

THE CAPO'S MISTRESS

"Something like that," I said. "But why didn't you just go to another casino? You said you were a good dealer and drew players to your table. You could find work anyplace there."

She looked down and played with her oatmeal before she said, "I would have been arrested if I stayed there."

The silence hung in the air. She was wanted in Vegas, probably for scamming the table, and my dream of a little house with a white picket fence and her in the kitchen baking a peach pie for dinner was falling apart. Wait a minute, I said to myself, so she's not perfect. I'm the guy who wasn't going to tell her until later that I was a drunk, so who's kidding who.

"What did you do?" I finally asked.

"I told you it's a long story," she said slowly. "How about picking up something for dinner and I'll tell you then?"

She wasn't happy anymore and I wanted her back the way she was in the bedroom, laughing and teasing me, and I kicked myself for bringing her down.

"Let's celebrate tonight," I said. "I'll take you out to dinner. It's your last day on the job and tomorrow we can stay in bed all day. That calls for a celebration. You pick the place."

The smile returned and she laughed and said, "How about Curly's? It's about the only place in town that will be open, and on Sunday night they have music and dancing."

"If you're fixin' to take me dancing, ma'am," I said in my best cowboy accent, "you're going to be mighty disappointed."

"We'll see about that," she said as she looked at her watch, then jumped up from the table and ran into the bedroom. "I've got to hurry or I'll be late."

She was only gone a few seconds before she reappeared with the engineer's cap on, gave me a kiss at the table, grabbed an umbrella and was out the door, leaving me alone in the house, already missing her. I spent the time doing some serious thinking about our future, which is the way I was already thinking of her, about who I was and about who she was.

I acknowledged that I had known her less than twenty-four hours but what the hell, she was the one for me, I told myself, then that nagging little voice I knew was coming asked if I wasn't just feeling the effects of a wonderful night in the sack that she had probably handed out to lots of other guys. The curse of the male psyche had me in its miserable grip. I didn't expect a virgin but I longed to know how many other men there had been and whether this was just another one night stand for her. Stop it, I told myself, what about yourself and the whores who paid you off in kind, how many of them had there been?

But I couldn't stop, to hell with political correctness, it was different for a man. I had planned to try to get in her pants from the minute we met, that's what men do, even though I didn't think I had a chance with her because she was so young and so beautiful. I was going through the motions, having fun thinking about it, when all of a sudden it happened. It's called getting lucky.

Couldn't we let well enough alone, I asked myself as if I was talking to another person. It had happened. Maybe she was as attracted to me as I was to her, maybe we were meant for each other. I started to laugh at the thought. You're a great kidder, I told myself. Look in the mirror. Who would be attracted to you? Now wait a minute, I argued back, I'm not the catch of the year but I'm not that bad, she's all alone, I might have looked good to her.

She told you she's all alone by choice, you idiot, because she got sick of guys fighting over her. She probably took pity on you and your pathetic dreams and granted your wish to give you something to think about in your old age; and speaking of guys fighting over her, it should be pretty obvious, even to a boob like you, that they were both getting into her and that's what the fight was about. That's the girl of your dreams, you dickhead, think about it.

THE CAPO'S MISTRESS

I had myself down for the count but I still wasn't satisfied so I asked myself, What about that crap about getting arrested if she went back to Vegas? What was that all about? She's not only sleeping with every man in town but she probably scammed the casino out of plenty and has it stashed away someplace, maybe here. If that's what you think, why don't you look around for it, I shot back, you're the big cop who can't handle his liquor. That made me mad, there was no reason to drag my drinking problem into the argument. Okay, I will, I said to myself. I hope you're satisfied.

I gave the house a good going over, looking for cash or jewelry or fancy clothes, and when I found nothing I hated myself for doubting her and for what I had done. Would she ever forgive me if she found out? Why should she? I had broken her trust and that was unforgivable. What in hell is the matter with you, I asked myself, you destroy everything that you touch. I had no answer.

The sun came out around noon and filled the house with its brightness. Maybe the gloomy day and being alone and missing her had gotten me down or maybe it was just me doing my usual number on myself, but I was low and I had to see her. I decided to go to the market and pick up some deli sandwiches and coffee for both of us and have lunch with her.

When I opened the door of the house I was unprepared for what I saw. It had gotten colder and the last of the rain had turned to snow, lightly dusting everything in white. To someone born and raised in L.A., where you had to drive at least a couple of hours to find snow, it was magical. There were no footprints, no tire tracks, nothing to mar the beauty of the scene before me, and I stood there in awe, afraid to move and destroy this moment. My spirits soared. The snow was pristine, like the beautiful and wondrous woman awaiting me, and I wanted to hold her and press her to me and never let her go.

I picked up the sandwiches and coffee and almost skipped down the street, through the few snowflakes, to my beloved, happiness all over my face. She saw me coming and opened the door to the little booth, laughing at the sight.

"I was just thinking about you," she said.

"I was thinking about you, too, and couldn't stay away any longer. May I take you to lunch?"

I held out the deli bag full of sandwiches and coffee.

"In the dining car, looking out the window of our train, it sounds heavenly," she replied. "Follow me."

She led me to a dining car that had been set up as an exhibit, the tables laden with china and silver and candles and also a coating of dust. In the twinkling of an eye she had wiped off the china with a damask napkin, arranged the sandwiches on dinner plates and poured the coffee. I held out her chair for her and we were at our table on the Orient Express bound from Paris to Istanbul. I told her our destination and she was thrilled.

"I've always wanted to see Istanbul," she said. "Are we on our honeymoon?"

"Yes," I said. "Last night we were married in Paris and we spent our first night together. It was wonderful."

"I remember," she said. "Do we have Pullman berths on the train?"

"Just one," I answered. "We're very poor but very much in love and I've spent all my money on our honeymoon."

She smiled dreamily. "Will you show me our berth after we've finished dining?"

"I will," I promised, and we bit into our deli sandwiches.

I walked back to the house on a cloud, lost in a dream of our life together, all doubts erased. She was it, the one, the only one, the forever after one. I was the luckiest man alive. I walked around the little house when I got there and tried to figure out where the posts for a white picket fence would go. It would be the happiest home in Virginia City.

chapter three

Curly's was mostly empty when we arrived and the music hadn't started. It was a big barn of a place, either made to look like or actually made out of logs, I couldn't tell which, with heads of buffalo, moose, and elk on the walls. There was a long bar, a few pool tables, and a small dance floor. Over the dance floor a big wagon wheel had been turned into a chandelier. All the tables were covered with red and white gingham tablecloths and there were a few waitresses standing around with short skirts and red and white gingham aprons.

Mary wore boots with a blue denim dress that almost reached the floor and silver buttons that buttoned up the front, an Indian silver necklace with a blue-green stone picking up the color of her eyes and a single eagle feather in her blonde hair. I went through the duffel bag and managed to find a reasonably clean shirt, jeans, and a pair of boots that I had bought for the trip.

We had steaks and a bottle of wine, most of it intended for her, and took our time, enjoying each other's company and taking a bite now and then. I know I looked sick with love for her and, while women never look that way, at least in public, I could tell she was having a good time being with me. The band started up, one guy on a keyboard who also sang from time to time, and the place got busy. Mary tried to teach me the mysteries of the two-step and at least I didn't embarrass myself while I waited for a slow one. We danced, returned to the table for some dinner, then danced some more until the set was over and the one-man band took a break.

I had a piece of steak up to my mouth when Mary suddenly said, "Let's go," and grabbed her purse.

I put my fork down and asked what the matter was, thinking I had offended her in some way, and that you could never figure out a woman.

"He's here," she said almost in panic, "up at the bar."

"Who's here?" I asked, not understanding her at all.

"The fellow who had a fight over me and punched me in the eye," she said. "Let's go before he sees us."

At first I was madder at her than at him, to think that she thought I would run away from some bozo who had socked the woman I loved; then my anger started to grow at him and I asked, "Where is he?"

"At the end of the bar, the tall one," she said. "Don't let him see me."

She was terrified and that made me angrier. I turned to look and wondered if I could pick him out of the crowd but I had no trouble and knew right away who it had to be. My old buddy the tow truck driver, Jeb Breckenridge, was holding court at the end of the bar with a bunch of hangers on. He hadn't seen us yet, but then the music started up again and he looked around the room to assess who was there for him to dance with and what lucky lady would have the pleasure of his company. I saw him stop when he spotted Mary with a date, and he started toward us, but I don't think he recognized me yet.

"Oh, my God, he's coming to the table," she said. "I've got to get out of here."

She started to stand and I pulled her back down.

"Running never solves anything," I said.

He was at the table now and asked her, without once looking at me, "Would you like to dance, Mary?"

"No, thank you, Jeb, I'm with someone," she answered.

"He doesn't mind, do you, buddy?" he asked, meaning he'd better not mind, and turned to me.

"As a matter of fact, I do mind, so why don't you leave us alone?" I replied, at the same time sizing Jeb up.

He was about two inches taller than I, a good ten years younger and he weighed close to 250 pounds, but I could see a lot of that was fat and he looked a bit like I used to look when I was on the booze. He was strong as hell, I could see that, but he was also slow, I thought, and that would help. I moved to the edge of the booth so I could get up quickly. The anger in me was boiling over and I wanted to kill him, when I saw the size of him, for hitting Mary or any woman.

He finally recognized me and turned back to Mary and grabbed her hand to pull her onto the dance floor.

"I thought you said you were with someone," he said. "He's from California, he's not a man."

"I'm glad that's what you think," I said, "because I hear you won't fight with men."

He turned and swung at me awkwardly because I was sitting down and he had to throw the punch across the table. I dodged it easily and, while I was still sitting down, hooked the toe of my left boot behind his right foot and drove my right boot into his right knee as hard as I could. He fell backward in a heap and I got out from behind the table and to my feet just as he got up and charged me as I expected him to do. I stepped to one side, slipped under his right fist and grabbed his right arm, then rolled him over my hip, using his own weight and the force of his charge against him. As he was coming down I put my knee under the right arm I was still holding and drove the arm against my knee with all my might, feeling and hearing it crack as it gave way. He screamed and got to his feet, heading for the door on a stream of curses, and I let him go.

It all happened so fast no one had time to intervene, or try to, and when he got out the door the room was very still and I stood there alone on the dance floor. I rejoined Mary at the table and the one-man band started to play again and things settled down and a few couples came onto the floor to dance. I asked the waitress for the check and was getting out my credit card when Jeb reappeared in the doorway with a shotgun under his left arm, and everyone dived for the floor as he raised the shotgun and pointed it in my direction. I pushed Mary under the table as the first barrel went off, taking out a buffalo head on the wall behind me and confirming my belief that, by the way he held the gun, Jeb wasn't left-handed. Probably the safest place to be was directly in front of him. I charged him and heard the sound of the second barrel going off and breaking glass as he nailed the bar mirror. I hit him with a rolling block and he fell onto the broken right arm, screaming in pain. I didn't care; now I was really mad and I kicked him in the ribs with my boot and felt something break, then grabbed his greasy hair and used it to pound his face into a bloody pulp on the dance floor until I was pulled off him and he was dragged into the kitchen by the bartender and a busboy in an unconcerned sort of way, as if they were sweeping the floor and this happened every night at Curly's.

I had lost it and beat the shit out of him. Five would have been proud of me. I went back to the table again to wait for the check and a funny thing happened. One or two guys came over to shake my hand and introduce themselves and, when the waitress brought the check, she let her hand linger on my shoulder way too long, which Mary picked up on immediately.

She was all of twenty-six or twenty-seven and had ignored me completely when she took our orders. Then a couple of girls dressed in flirty skirts for the dance sauntered by and gave me the once over and it suddenly hit me. I had defeated the Bull Moose and I was the new leader of the herd, at least in Curly's, and all the females belonged to me and all the males would do my bidding. I was the new Bull Moose, the king of the hill, and I couldn't hold back a little smile of satisfaction, which Mary also picked up on, because women are like that and can sense the slightest threat to their position of pre-eminence.

"Let's get out of here," she said, and I thought about saying that I wanted to stay awhile with my herd, but I didn't want to ruin her mood so I said okay.

We were both turned on by the evening and the excitement and the smell of blood in the air, and when we got outside we couldn't wait until we got back to the house and started in right there. We had walked to Curly's and it was too cold and wet for the bushes so I started to try the doors of cars in the parking lot, both of us growing more and more needy with each grope and each locked door, until I finally spotted a Crown Victoria about ten years old, like we used to drive on patrol in L.A. No one would lock that piece of crap, I thought, and I was right. We fell on top of each other in the back seat like dogs going after a piece of meat.

It was cold on the walk back home and I asked what had happened to the car she came here in.

"It's in the garage in back of the house," she answered, as if that explained everything.

"Then why did you walk to work this morning in the rain?"

"I'm about six months behind to the finance company," she replied, "and I don't want them to spot it so I leave it in the garage. If I have to get out of here in a hurry I'll need that car."

"Oh, yeah," he replied. "He gets into fights all the time at Curly's. Doesn't usually shoot up the place, though, that's why I have to make a report. Damn nuisance." He winked at me, one officer to another, and added, "I suppose you know."

"Sure do," I agreed, "just retired after thirty years on the force."

He whistled. "That's a lot of years. What are you doing now?"

"Nothing yet, just looking around, I came up here to visit my old partner at Henry's Lake in Idaho. He wanted me to retire there."

Mary came into the room and called him Bob and he called her Mary and they shook hands. She excused herself to make coffee and Mary's buddy Bob asked me to tell him what happened last night and how the fight had started. When I had finished he said that was pretty much the story he got at Curly's and asked if I wanted to press charges against Jeb for taking a couple of shots at me with his shotgun. I said to forget about it just as Mary came in with the coffee. She poured us each a cup and took a cup for herself and sat down. I could see he couldn't figure out the relationship between me and Mary, so I told him about my car breaking down and that my money was low and how I met her at the train depot and she took pity on me and offered me bed on the sofa and breakfast for $25 a night.

"I was happy to do it," Mary chipped in. "My rent comes due this week."

"How about you, Mary," he asked her, "do you want to file a complaint against Jeb?"

"No," she answered, "I just want him to leave me alone."

"Did you file against him when he socked you?" I asked, thinking maybe she should get a restraining order against him.

"No," she answered quietly.

"I never heard about that," the sheriff joined in. "When

did that happen?"

"When Jeb had that fight with Roy about four or five months ago and put him in the hospital," she replied.

"I remember that," Sheriff Bob said, "because I had to do a report on account of the injuries, but I don't remember anything about him hitting you."

"It was later," Mary explained, "and I didn't report it because I was afraid of him."

"The doctor says it'll be a couple of days before he's up and around again and I'll tell him to stay away from you," the sheriff said, and finished his coffee.

He stood up to leave and thanked us both for our cooperation. I walked him to the door and out of the blue he asked if I might be interested in coming to work for him. I didn't know what to say but I knew I didn't want to flat out turn him down, so I asked if I could think it over and let him know.

"Take your time," he said, shaking my hand again. "We need another man but I'm willing to wait awhile for someone who can handle himself like you did against Jeb. I still don't know how you did it. He's a mean son of a bitch."

He turned and walked down the porch steps, leaving me speechless.

I told Mary about the offer, proud of myself, and asked whether she would like to live with me in her little house in Virginia City, Montana for the rest of our lives and that I would put a white picket fence around it and we would be very happy.

"I thought you wanted me to come to Los Angeles with you," she said. "I hate it here. In the winter everybody leaves. It's a real ghost town then, only about 150 people live here full time."

"It was just a thought," I said, crushed by her reply.

She saw that she had hurt me and put her hand on my shoulder.

THE CAPO'S MISTRESS

"Let's get another cup of coffee and sit down. It's time we had that talk."

She got the coffee pot and we sat on the sofa in front of the fireplace. I looked at her, waiting.

"I'm in a lot of trouble," she began. "Let me tell you how it happened and then you can tell me what to do about it. I was dealing blackjack on the evening shift and had just come on duty. It was a Tuesday night and Tuesdays are usually slow, especially early, and there were only one or two players at my table when all of a sudden all hell broke loose. Three men had gotten into the cashier's cage somehow, they thought later it was an inside job, and were holding it up, but I didn't know it at the time and was just dealing to the players at the table. They scooped all the money and chips into bags and then ran for the door but someone gave the alarm before they got out of the casino and the guards came after them. They tried to shoot their way out and the guards shot back and everyone hit the floor or ran for the exits but me. I was scared to death and just froze when the shooting started and couldn't move. One of the robbers ran right by me and he had already been shot and was covered with blood and I think he knew he was going to die because he looked at me and said, clear as day, 'Have fun, blondie,' and dropped the bag he was carrying right at my feet and kept on running. I knew it was full of money and I don't know why I did it but I kicked it under the table and threw my coat on top of it. The casino was going crazy and everyone was running for the doors, even the pit bosses, and I thought the bosses looking down from above us were probably freaked out too, so I picked up the bag with my coat over it and ran for the door. When I got outside I didn't know what to do with the bag and then I saw the Treasure Island lagoon and I ran over to it. Everyone had left the lagoon to see what the excitement was all about so I counted down three vertical railings from the end closest to the pirate ship and I threw the bag in and it sank like a rock."

She paused for breath, exhausted from the effort of telling her story and excited by it too.

"What's the Treasure Island lagoon?" I asked dumbly. "I haven't been to Vegas for years. I gave up gambling a long time ago." Except for the $200 I lost at Five's place, I thought.

"It's like a tourist attraction," she answered. "There's a pirate ship and an English ship in a big lagoon and they fight each other. It's free and they run it a lot of times every night to attract the tourists. The idea is that when the show is over they'll go into the casino to gamble. Some do, some don't, a lot of the watchers are families with kids."

"So what did you do after you threw the bag in the lagoon?" I asked.

"I went back into the casino and asked if we were closing because of the robbery and the bodies that were still there, and they told me they were just going to close off that area because they didn't want to lose all the business from the saps that had come in to see what was going on, and that they would move me to another table and I was to work my regular shift until two a.m., so I did."

I asked her what happened to the bag of money that she threw in the lagoon and was that how she got into trouble, not yet able to figure why she would be arrested if she went back to Vegas, and she took my hand and looked down at her hand in mine.

"I don't know how to tell you this," she said, "because you might just get up and walk out, and I wouldn't blame you, but I don't want to lose you."

Oh, oh, I thought, I'm not going to like this, and said, "Just go ahead and tell it, that's the best way, it can't be anything I haven't heard a million times before as a cop," but feeling more like a priest.

"Well," she said, "I told you I had a lot of players that

were attracted to my table, but some of them were special and always visited my table when they were in town, but not just to play blackjack, if you know what I mean."

Jesus Christ, she's a hooker, I thought, and felt like Jeb had just landed a solid right hand to my stomach. I wanted to throw up, I wanted to hit her, I wanted to hit myself until I was unconscious, I wanted to die, but instead I said, "I think I do."

"It's not like I was a hooker," she said, and I wondered why not. "I had known some of them for years and sometimes, when they had won big, they would give me a big tip and ask if I would like to get together after work. Sometimes I said 'yes' and sometimes I said 'no,' it depended on my mood, and if it sounded good to me I said 'yes.' Would it surprise you if I told you I enjoy sex?"

"No," I said, "it wouldn't," and smiled despite myself, remembering how she conquered and humiliated the dirty little coward, but I had to go on. Men are like that when the subject is the chastity of the woman they love, and so I asked how many of her "special" players there were.

She looked hurt but said about ten or fifteen, and I thought, Jesus Christ, calling on Him again for the answer, doesn't she even know the number, what does it take to be "special" other than being a big winner at the table? I couldn't stop, the answer was going to hurt me, I knew, but I had to ask the question, "How much did you charge your friends?"

I shouldn't have added "your friends." I knew it was cruel and hurtful when I said it, but I wanted to hurt her, how dare she be a whore. The white picket fence was being torn down along with all my dreams of our life together.

She took it as cruel and wanted to hurt me back, so she looked me straight in the eye and said without blinking, "Five hundred dollars, sometimes more for something special."

She hurt me all right, bad, but I had asked for it and I

thought, who the hell am I to judge her, I couldn't look her in the eye as she had done and tell her about my past. I felt dirty and mean and small.

I put my arms around her and held her and said, "I'm sorry, it's just that I don't want there to be anyone else."

She looked at me with her incredible green eyes and said simply, "There isn't."

What beautiful words. They washed away all the anger and hurt and made me feel wonderful again. Then she said, "Please let me get this over with," and I sat back to listen.

"Anyway, when my shift was up, there was a friend of mine at the table and he walked away from the table with me and told me he had to catch a flight at six in the morning for New York and he didn't feel like going to sleep and would I like to come to his room for a nightcap. He was staying at the Venetian and I said that I would so we went up to his room and partied. When it was time for him to leave he said for me to just stay there and catch some sleep, so I did, and when I woke up at around eleven I turned on the TV to hear about the robbery the night before and there was my picture big as life. I had forgotten about the surveillance cameras and they had tape of the robber throwing me the bag and me taking the bag outside wrapped in my coat and they said that I was not at home and hadn't been seen since my shift was over at 2 a.m. The reporter said that there was speculation that the robbery had been set up by someone working inside the casino and the police theory was that it was me."

She took time out for a sip of coffee and then continued. "I was scared to death. I had taken the bag full of money and hidden it and they had me on tape doing it, at least as far as the door. I couldn't go home, they'd be waiting for me, and I didn't know what to do, so I took a shower and got dressed and tried to cover my face as best I could. My car was in the parking lot at the Treasure Island and my only chance was that if my car hadn't been identified and if I made it to the car I could get out of town. I did and the rest is history. Now what do I do?"

"Do you know how much was in the bag?" I asked.

"The TV reporter said the other bags had been recovered and the amount in the missing bag was estimated at between two and three hundred thousand dollars."

I whistled, then said, "Well, if they get you as a co-conspirator, or even an accessory, the felony-murder rule takes over and you're looking at life in prison; that is, if the jury doesn't believe your story that you had no part in the robbery. If the jury does buy your story, you're guilty of grand theft, at least, and you're probably looking at twenty-five years."

She started to cry. "What am I going to do? What am I going to do?" she asked over and over. "I can't give myself up. I can't go to prison. Please help me."

"I will," I said.

Hell, I told myself, I had helped Five out plenty of times and I didn't even like him. I loved her.

She stopped crying and looked at me, then said, "What are we going to do?"

I noticed the "we" right away. I was on board, hook, line and sinker.

"We're going to go to L.A. and get married, if you'll have me, and we're going to live happily ever after. I'll be just another retired cop and you'll be my very beautiful wife and the only question that will ever be asked is, What does she see in him?"

She laughed and kissed me. "If that's a proposal, I accept. It's a beautiful day. Let's get some sandwiches and a bottle of champagne and go on a picnic to celebrate."

We walked outside. The snow on the ground had melted and the sky was a kind of transparent blue, it had a depth to it so that it seemed you were looking through one blue sky at another and another. A few white clouds, just puffs of white, were scattered around the sky haphazardly and the mountains in the distance were shades of purple made by the different ways the sun hit them. There was a chill in the air that made my skin feel clean, I don't know why but that was the feeling it gave me. I looked at the old houses of Virginia City around me and Old Town in the distance and I felt that I was home. I never wanted to leave here. I turned to Mary. She had pulled on the big floppy sweater and jeans she was wearing when I first saw her, but not the railroad cap, and her blonde hair was blowing around her face in the wind. What does she see in me, I asked myself, and the answer came back, just shut up and count your blessings.

I looked again at the purple mountains in the distance. "Let's find a spot where we'll be all alone. I don't have a car. Can we use yours?"

"I told you I'm afraid of the finance company. Let's borrow one from Sam," and we headed for the deli arm in arm, smiles covering both our faces. I was thinking how our picnic would wind up and that explained the smile on my face. I don't know about Mary.

chapter four

Sam looked up from his newspaper when we came into the garage loaded down with the makings of a wonderful picnic.

"Well, lookee here," he said. "What are you two up to?"

Mary smiled dazzlingly. "We're going on a picnic, Sam, and we hoped we could borrow a car from you if Mike's isn't ready."

I looked at the old clunker standing forlornly in the corner of the garage like a horse with a broken leg. Mike's car sure as hell wasn't ready and not another car was in sight. Sam looked sick. I knew he wanted to help us but he couldn't.

"Sorry, Mary, the only car here that works is mine. Where did you want to go?"

"I don't know, someplace pretty, can you suggest something?"

Sam brightened. "Alder Gulch, and historic too. Did you know that's where they first struck gold?"

He didn't give Mary a chance to answer.

"A fellow named Bill Fairweather and some of his friends were captured by Indians and taken to a Crow village. Believe me, they were mighty scared. The Crow chief told them he would let them go if they went back where they came from and got out of Crow territory. They didn't know exactly what was Crow territory so they traveled by night and kept to the ridges. They camped in a creek bottom where they were hidden by a bunch of alders to cook dinner. After dinner Bill stuck his shovel into the gravel to see if he could find enough gold for 'tobacco money' and hit pay dirt. They mined $10,000,000 the first year."

"That's quite a story, Sam," I said when he stopped talking.

"Oh, there's more," Sam said. "Tell you what, why don't we all climb into my car and I'll take you to Alder. Don't worry, I'll leave you alone while you picnic. There's a place called Robber's Roost that you ought to see. It's an old saloon where hold-up gangs used to hang out in the gold rush days to rob stagecoaches making the run between Bannack and Virginia City. I'll get something to eat there while you're having your picnic."

Having Sam along was not what I had in mind for fun on the picnic, and I was about to tell him so when Mary said, "Oh, Sam, that's so kind of you, but you would have to close the garage."

I think she was thinking the same thing I was but it never dawned on Sam.

"It's no trouble at all, Mary, nobody's going to come in anyway and I get a kick out of telling strangers about Virginia City. It'll be my pleasure."

He walked to his car and drove it over to where we were standing and opened the rear doors for us. "You two ride along in back and I'll be the tour guide for us. No trouble at all."

We looked at each other and Mary kind of held up the

palms of her hands where Sam couldn't see, as if to say, what can we do? Sam took up the story again as we drove out of town.

"Remember I told you how Bill Fairweather stuck his shovel into Alder Creek and discovered gold, well, that's how Virginia City got its start. When Bill and his friends got back to Bannack they couldn't keep their mouths shut, and when they left town with more supplies over two hundred people were following them. When they all got to the strike they called a miners' meeting to set up rules for staking claims, and they laid out a town site a mile below the strike and called it Varina and that's how Virginia City got its start. Within a year the population was over ten thousand. They lived in tents and shacks and every third building was a saloon complete with— excuse me, Mary—whores. In 1865 Virginia City became the territorial capital. How about that?"

He stopped, obviously pleased with himself and his story.

"Sam, do you know I never heard of Virginia City, Montana before my car broke down?" I asked. "I thought the only one was in Nevada."

"Most people say that," he answered. "Have you ever heard of Mark Twain?"

He looked at me in the rear view mirror. It was a rhetorical question and I nodded.

"He was in the Confederate Army and he deserted and came here for a while before he went to Virginia City, Nevada, where he got better known. They shipped silver to the south during the Civil War the same as Virginia City, Montana sent gold to the south. They were both Confederate towns. How about Jeremiah Johnson? Ever hear of him?"

"Sure, the mountain man," I answered.

"Well, he was in Virginia City during the winter of 1863 looking for Wolf, the chief of the Blackfeet. He attacked Wolf's camp north of Virginia City with his mountain men and killed seventy Blackfeet and left Wolf's head in the middle of the trail. Later he became the sheriff of Red Lodge."

Sam fell quiet and I didn't want to start him up again so I was quiet too. Mary was looking out the window of the car at the trees and patches of snow along the road and looked bored. I had the feeling she would much rather be looking at the hotels and excitement of Las Vegas, and I squeezed her hand. She smiled wanly and turned back to the window.

After a while Sam said we were coming into Alder and he drove us to the Robber's Roost, which was an old saloon sure enough, but right in the middle of a farm. It had an antique store and museum and reminded me of the old locomotives at the Railroad Museum in Virginia City. It was no longer being used for the purpose intended, a place to get drunk or get laid or have a gunfight. It was a pallid replica of its old self. Then it hit me, and the thought really brought me down. It was me. I was the old locomotive left out to rot in the sun and the rain and the snow, I was the Robber's Roost saloon, sitting in a farmyard, a relic of a bygone era. Once I had been a cop, not a very good one for the most part, but the last eight years I was proud of, now I'm discarded, too old, too outmoded, retired. What an ugly word. I didn't want to be retired, I wanted to be on active duty, facing up to the bad guys and protecting the good guys, getting shot at and shooting back, a good cop for the rest of my life. The job offer from the sheriff was too good to be true. I wanted that job. I wanted to live in Virginia City for the rest of my life, in the little house with Mary, the one I was going to build a white picket fence around. She would change her mind and live here with me, I knew it, I don't know how, I just knew it. I was happy again.

I grabbed Mary and kissed her. She looked surprised. We left Sam in the Robber's Roost and got the picnic basket out of the car. Mary spread a blanket on the ground while I popped the cork on the champagne. It was a wonderful picnic. We were alone at last even though we were in a field just outside the Robber's Roost, and maybe being alone together was what made it wonderful, but the sky was still that transparent Montana blue with little puffs of white in it and the nip in the weather made my skin feel clean. The only thing I missed was how I thought the picnic would wind up when we started out from the little house, and that wasn't going to happen on a blanket outside the Robbers' Roost. I would have to wait until we got home for that. We talked happily about a lot of things but not a word was said about Mary staying in Virginia City. That too would have to wait for another time and place.

Sam came out after a respectful time for us to enjoy the picnic and each other and we got in his car. On the way back to Virginia City he started in again on the gold rush and the Civil War and the vigilantes.

I was feeling the champagne, and while Sam was droning on, I put my hand on Mary's blue jeans and moved it up her thigh. She shook her head no and nodded to Sam in the front seat but I just moved the hand up higher. She shook her head again and took the hand away but I put it back, higher still.

She leaned over and whispered in my ear, "No, and I mean it, not in front of Sam."

I whispered back, "It's not in front of Sam, it's in back of Sam, and it's just a little foreplay for what's waiting for you when you get home."

"Lucky me," she whispered back. "I told you no and I meant it, I'm not going to have him telling everyone in town what went on in his back seat."

She took my hand away again and I put it back.

"Stop it," she whispered angrily, "you're drunk."

Though she couldn't know the effect her words would have on me, it was like a slap in the face or a bucket of cold water in the middle of a hot shower. I hadn't heard those words for almost eight years. She was right, I had been careless, no longer concerned about staying sober so I could get her into bed, that was now a foregone conclusion, and the champagne had tasted so good I had most of the bottle. I pulled the offending hand back and we rode the rest of the way in silence. She probably thought I was pouting but it wasn't that at all. I was beating myself up for letting the booze get to me. It had snuck up on me like the proverbial thief in the night and I had made an ass of myself in the guise of being the life of the party, making jokes about not being in front of Sam but in back of him and telling Mary that I wanted to warm her up with a little foreplay for what was coming when we got home. Women do not like drunks, even funny ones, and especially those who think they're funny but aren't funny at all.

Sam let us out in front of the little house and we thanked him for his hospitality, then Mary asked Sam if he'd like to come in for a drink. It was payback time. She might as well have said I know what you have on your mind, funnyman, and if you had paid attention to me in the car we'd be heading for the sack, but now that isn't going to happen. My only hope was that Sam would have the good sense to call it a day.

Sam said a drink sounded mighty good to him and that he had a few more stories about Virginia City to tell.

chapter five

Tuesday it was raining again and we had a late breakfast, toying with our food and mooning at each other. Suddenly she put down her coffee cup and asked, "What are we going to do about the money?"

"What money?" I asked, but knowing where this conversation was going.

"In the bag in the lagoon," she said, looking at me in a way that suggested that she had serious doubts about my competency.

"Just leave it there. Sooner or later they'll clean the lagoon and find it," I said.

"Whoever finds it will keep it," she said angrily, "and that's my money. He gave it to me."

"It wasn't his to give," I pointed out.

She looked at me in disbelief and said, "Do you mean you're going to pass up $300,000 that's just sitting there waiting for us to get it? I can't believe you. What kind of a man are you?"

I didn't like that question and answered, "One that doesn't want us to get caught and have you sent to a prison someplace where the warden is a dyke and will take one look at you and say there's a God in heaven after all."

"Look," she said, "I can draw a map showing right where it is, all you have to do is pull it out of the water."

I noticed that I was the designated puller-outer and said, "If it's so easy why haven't you done it?"

"I told you, I'm too well known. I was a dealer at the Treasure Island for years, I'd be recognized and arrested on the spot. No one will recognize you. Please get it. We'll be set for the rest of our lives. We can even buy this house, if you want to, and you can go to work for the sheriff and I'll be waiting for you when you come home."

She would live in Virginia City with me and I would be the deputy sheriff, that's what she had said. The white picket fence was up again, looking good. All I had to do was get the bag out of the lagoon.

"How deep is the water in the lagoon?" I asked, almost against my will.

"I don't know," she said. "There are concrete walls around the lagoon and the water is about six feet below street level. The bottom is probably five or six feet below that to hide the rails the ships run on."

I thought for a minute and then said half to myself, "I'd have to do it around three or four in the morning to minimize the chance of being spotted, so I'll need a face mask and a waterproof flashlight to find the damn bag. I could wear sweats with a wetsuit underneath and pretend to be jogging until I got to the lagoon. No, that's out. I've got to allow for the possibility that I'll get caught and the wetsuit is a giveaway that I came to look for something in the lagoon. So are the flashlight and the face mask."

I stopped and pondered.

"That's perfect," she said. "You did come to look for something in the lagoon. People throw money into it all the time. If you're caught you can say you lost all your money at the tables and you were trying to collect enough change for the bus fare home. There are a million hard luck stories in Las Vegas. Someone might even give you a few dollars."

"Maybe that explains the mask and the flashlight," I replied, "but not the wetsuit. Diving for change because you're broke is a desperation thing. Nobody comes to Vegas prepared for it. I'll have to do it in my sweats. Once I get out and away from there no one will give me a second glance because I'm running around in a wet sweat suit."

"What about the bag? You can't be caught with that," Mary said.

I hadn't thought about the bag and I could picture myself saying, "I was broke and I thought I would dive for some money and I hit the jackpot. Isn't that what you do in Las Vegas?"

I would deny knowing Mary or anything about her and I would be made as one of the robbers back to pick up the loot. I would go away for a long time and never see Mary again. This was getting complicated, and I picked up my coffee cup and pondered some more.

"It will have to be in two stages," I said finally. "The first night I'll locate the bag and tie something to it so I can pull it out quickly. I'll wear sweats and fill the pockets with change to back up the story that I was diving for money if I'm spotted. The second night I'll be dry as a bone and carry a suitcase or something else I can throw the bag into when I pull it out. It will be all over in less than a minute and I'll be walking nice and slow down the street gawking at all the big hotels like a tourist who just blew into town."

She threw her arms around me. "Then you'll do it?" she asked. There was only one answer to that question and she knew it.

"You sold me when you said we could buy this house and live here happily ever after," I replied. "I'd better go down to the garage and find out if the car will be ready tomorrow. It's a long way to Vegas."

I walked down the hill waiting for the voice. I knew it was coming and I knew the subject and I didn't know how to answer. The voice said, I thought you wanted to be a good cop, what happened? What do you mean, I answered, stalling for time, I'll be the best damn deputy sheriff Bob Hill ever saw. By stealing $250,000 to get started? the voice asked. I'm not stealing anything, I answered, the money is there in the lagoon waiting to be picked up.

You mean like a sack of money that drops off a Brink's truck, that's free game? No, not like that at all. This money was stolen from all the poor saps that played the slots and the other games in the casino, all fixed for the house. Believe me, they'd want me to have it if they can't get it back, and they sure as hell can't. Interesting theory, the voice said, is that the law that you're sworn to uphold?

That got me mad. You know damn well it isn't, I answered, what I'm doing is called jury nullification: in a particular setting, under a particular set of facts, the law doesn't fit and reasonable people know that and take the law into their own hands to achieve justice. The voice gave a smug chuckle, so help me, and asked, what is the particular justice you propose to achieve here? Is it, perchance, that you and Mary be enriched by $250,000 that you didn't earn? No, no, no, I yelled, it's that Mary and I be saved, resurrected from our miserable lives to redeem ourselves by hard work and helping others. The voice was laughing now as it asked, do you need $250,000 to do that? Did the sheriff say he would hire you if you gave him $250,000?

No, I answered, but I'm not going to take the job if Mary

isn't with me and she wants the money or we'll go to L.A. Is that something like Hell? the voice asked in a snotty tone. *You go to hell,* I answered, I'm in love for the first time in a long time and it's wonderful and I'm going to do what it takes to live in Virginia City with Mary and be the best damn deputy sheriff I can be. It's as simple as that. At least you're leveling with me, the voice said, and was gone.

    Sam Culpepper was sitting in his office reading the paper. The garage was empty except for my clunker and it looked the same as yesterday. He put down the paper and stood up, holding out his hand to me.

    "How are you, young fellow," he began. "I didn't want to mention it in front of Mary, but I hear you had a run-in with Jeb Breckenridge at Curly's. Wish I could have been there to see it."

    I ignored the topic and asked, "How's the car coming?"

    "I've got some bad news," Sam said, looking glum. "The parts haven't arrived yet. They didn't have them in stock in Helena so they're on order. I probably won't get them until next Monday. There wasn't anything I could do. Sorry about that."

    I was no longer dismayed at the thought of being stuck in Virginia City so I couldn't really get mad at Sam.

    "When will the car be ready if you get the parts on Monday?" I asked.

    "I'll have it ready for you late Tuesday or Wednesday morning for sure," Sam replied with a big smile. "I want to get you out of town before Jeb finds you."

    "Ain't gonna be no rematch," I replied.

    "I'm not talking about that," Sam said, then added, "Jeb's got a real mean streak. No telling what he might do to even the score with you. You showed him up in front of all his friends. He's gonna want to pay you back in spades, mark my words. It's a good thing you're not gonna be around here much longer."

"I might be here for quite a while, as it turns out," I said.

He looked at me. "Mary?" he asked.

"Maybe," I replied.

Sam whistled. "That's even worse," Sam said. "Jeb's had a thing for her ever since she came to town. It already caused some trouble. Take my advice and watch your back."

"Thanks, I will," I said and walked out of his office and back to the little house.

"Take my car," Mary said when she heard about the delay.

"What about the finance company?" I asked.

"Can't you swap the plates on your car? No one will notice a Mercedes with California plates in Vegas. There are millions of them," she said.

So it's a Mercedes, I thought, and then said, "Let's have a look at your car."

We went out to the garage. I expected one of the bottom of the line models that people who don't have a pot to piss in buy so they can say they drive a Mercedes and I was disappointed that Mary was one of them, but she opened the garage door to the top of the line, bright red, with a price tag of somewhere between one hundred and two hundred thousand dollars. I could see why she didn't want to drive it around town, and it had nothing to do with the finance company even if they were looking for the car. It would cause talk, lots of it, that the ticket taker at the railroad museum tooled around town in a car that the president of the local bank couldn't afford.

I whistled and said, "That's some car," leaving the question unasked as to how she happened to have it in her garage, paid for or not, and thinking to myself that she must have been more than a casual hooker in Vegas to make that kind of money. The unasked question hung in the air and she read my dirty mind.

"When I was working in Vegas I could afford it but not here," she said, leaving the kind of work in Vegas deliberately vague and leaving me in agony wondering how much she had made as a blackjack dealer and how much she had made on her back. Did I really want to do this, I asked myself? Was she worth the risk I was about to take? I had known her for less than four days and I was in love with her, there was no question about that, but did she love me or was this all a con?

She sensed my hesitation and, as only women can do, put her arms around me and said, "We'll be so happy here in our little house. I love you so."

She looked up at me from her incredible green eyes and suddenly the risk didn't matter to me, she had said she loved me and that was enough, who was I to question it, why should I question it, she loved me and I loved her, that was all that mattered. I walked back to the garage and got the plates off the old clunker and put Mary's plates on. Sam of course wanted to know why, and I told him that there were a lot of people in Montana who didn't like Californians and, since I was going to be here for a while, or maybe forever, I thought I had better take the California plates off the car.

"Aw, Californians aren't all bad," he said, "just those pointy-headed liberals you've got out there. You seem like a nice enough person, for example. I'll bet you weren't born there."

"Born and raised in L.A.," I replied.

He thought for a minute. "I'll bet your folks came from someplace else," he said finally.

"Both from up-state New York," I answered, trying to help Sam make his point.

"You see," he replied, "if they were from New York City it would have been no different. They're just as bad as Californians. But being from upper New York state they knew how to raise you good and proper." He smiled that the world was right again. I took the California plates and told Sam I'd see him next week to pick up the car.

"See," he said, "you're starting to act like somebody from Montana already. Ain't no reason to hurry, right?"

I told him to take another week if he wanted to, and he picked up his paper again as I walked out of his office. I put the plates on Mary's car and decided I would leave for Vegas first thing in the morning. It was about 800 miles away and even in Mary's car, which was built for the autobahn, if I left at eight in the morning I wouldn't get in until around eight or nine Wednesday night. I figured I'd have time to look at the lagoon at night and try to work out a plan of attack, then go over it on Thursday in the daylight and actually go into the lagoon that night. If all went well I'd take the bag out of the lagoon Friday night and be on my way back to Mary on Saturday.

Last Saturday morning I was on my way to L.A. from Henry's Lake and hadn't even met Mary. What a lot can happen in a week. I packed the duffel bag and loaded it in the car and Mary drew a map of the lagoon and where the bag was. She wasn't much of a map maker but we went over it together and I got a pretty good idea of where she had dropped the bag into the lagoon. It was getting late and I suggested we go back to Curly's for our last dinner together as poor people. I didn't tell her that I wanted to visit my herd one more time before leaving town to see if I was still the head moose.

She looked at me and said slowly, with just a touch of sarcasm, "Oh, did you like Curly's?"

She's too damn smart, I thought, and answered, "It was okay. You said it was the only place in town still open."

"Then Curly's it will be," she replied. "I've got to shower and get dressed for a night on the town."

When she finally was ready there was no doubt who would catch the eye of the new Bull Moose. She had gotten rid of the boots and blue denim dress, replaced by high heels and a short frilly number that showed a lot of leg, and her hair was twisted around on top of her head except for a few strands that dropped down loosely on each side of her face.

I whistled and said, "What are you trying to do, start another fight? Every man in the place will be drooling over you."

She gave me a long slow smile and said, "But I'll be going home with you," then sang softly, looking straight at me, "and when we get behind closed doors...." The melody trailed off but the thought lingered on. Suddenly I didn't want to go to Curly's at all and said so, but she would have none of it and threw a heavy coat over what she was wearing, which was almost nothing at all.

The herd gathered around the new Bull Moose when he appeared. The hostess called me Mike and said she would take us to our regular booth, if that was satisfactory, and when we were seated the same waitress introduced herself as Suzie, which she hadn't bothered to do before, and bent way over when she poured our water, showing some well-formed jugs of her own. The bartender brought over two glasses of champagne, compliments of the house, and while we were having dinner the couples dancing by were all smiles. The new Bull Moose was here and the herd was happy and properly deferential.

I offered to help Mary out of her coat when we first sat down but she wanted to keep it on, and I thought she was cold from our walk to Curly's but then one of the girls at the bar came over and asked me to dance, ignoring Mary. It was the situation of the other night in reverse and Mary said sweetly that the first dance belonged to her, she hoped the girl wouldn't mind, then stood and removed her coat and held out her hand to me. It was like the champ taking his robe off in the ring before the first round, the sight of the muscles and grace that had propelled him to the championship striking fear into the

Saturday.

"Aren't you going to phone me to tell me that you love me or how it's going?" she pouted.

"Nope," I explained, "in case I'm picked up I don't want to leave a record of telephone calls at the hotel or even on the cell phone, so don't try to reach me. It's the first thing the police will look for if they're trying to find you and figure I know where you are."

"You're so smart," she said with a smile.

"Flattery will get you anyplace you want with me," I replied, "so save it for when I come back, you might be horny."

"I'll try to be, so hurry back," she said and kissed me good-bye.

chapter six

I was used to the squad car or my old clunker and I got a kick out of flashing by other cars in the big red Mercedes, until I saw a police car parked ahead of me and I remembered that driving a fast red car by a traffic cop is like waving a red cape in front of a bull. I managed to get within the speed limit without laying down fifty feet of rubber and went by with my eyes straight ahead, then watched the police car in the rear view. It didn't move and I breathed a sigh of relief, thinking that I didn't have any registration for the car with me and they would run the plates and find that they didn't belong on the car I was driving. Even the copper-stopper wouldn't help me then. It was going to be a long slow drive to Vegas, within the speed limit, and I probably could have made better time with the clunker. What the hell, I'll use the time to go over the plan of attack and work out any kinks.

I was going to attach a rope to the bag on Thursday night and pull it out on Friday night. The first problem was the weight of the bag full of water, and I decided to allow one hundred pounds for it, probably overkill, but I would have to have a strong rope for sure. Next, how was I going to get the rope to the bag? I knew roughly where the bag was so there was no point in carrying the rope into the water with me. It made more sense to drop the rope into the water near the bag and swim to both of them, and that meant the rope would have to be white so I could spot it easily in the dark water with the flashlight. Then I remembered that the surface of the water was about six feet below the sidewalk, how would I reach the rope the next night to pull it out? I decided to tie one end of a piece of nylon fishing line to one end of the rope and the other end of the fish line to the bottom of the post where Mary had thrown the bag into the lagoon. It would be almost invisible, I hoped, and would not be spotted until I came to pull up the rope the next night. But how would I attach the other end of the rope to the bag once I found it? I couldn't trust the handle to hold the weight of the bag after being in the water so long, and I decided to buy one of those net sports bags and sink it with the rope tied to a handle of the sports bag. I would put the bag full of money in it, and then pull the whole mess up the next night and the water would drain out of the sports bag as I was pulling it up. To hell with the bag full of money, how was I going to get out of the lagoon myself once I had put it in the sports bag? This was getting ridiculous.

I didn't like the idea of climbing out on the pirate ship, which was supposed to be stationary, because it was bound to have alarms for idiots who wanted to get on the ship to have their pictures taken, so I would have to get out by climbing up the wall to the sidewalk. I decided to get another rope, this one dark, not white, knot it for climbing, tie it to another of the vertical pipes that were part of the railing, and use it to let myself down into the water without a splash, close to the location of the bag, then use it again to climb back out again and take it with me. The next night I would pull up the sports bag, put everything into a waterproof suitcase, and walk away gawking at the buildings like a tourist. I had a lot of shopping to do tomorrow.

That got me as far as Salt Lake City and I thought about stopping and trying to find an A.A. meeting but I decided against it. I had fallen off the wagon badly at Henry's Lake but that was behind me and I blamed Five and his buddies for it. True, I had continued to drink with Mary but I had kept it under control, except for a little too much champagne at the picnic, and that was a good sign. Maybe it was just Five that drove me off into binge drinking and I could handle beer and wine, or even a shot of the hard stuff, if he wasn't around. I knew what they would say about that theory at the A.A. meeting and I guess that's why I didn't stop, but I had been under control with Mary and that was a fact.

Fact my ass, I answered myself back, what about the picnic where you chug-a-lugged most of the bottle of champagne? The only reason you were under control with Mary is because you wanted to get laid more than you wanted to get drunk, and once you got laid you started to slop it down again, and that's a fact. Now wait a minute, I answered, it was only champagne, not the hard stuff, and we were celebrating, that's what champagne is for; it's like soda pop, I could drink it all night and not get high, and I had reason to celebrate, isn't Mary the most wonderful girl in the world?

What the hell does that have to do with anything, I asked, so she's wonderful, so what? The subject under discussion is whether you're a drunk, and all you've shown is that you can keep it under control when you want something more than you want booze, but when that passes you're the same old lush. Go to hell, I told myself. I pulled out Mary's lunch to stop the argument and nibbled as I drove.

It started to get dark and then got dark and I could see the lights of Las Vegas in the distance. I used to spend a lot of

THE CAPO'S MISTRESS

time and money there when I had it to spend, before I hit the skids really bad, but my last visit was about fifteen years ago and I wasn't prepared for what I was about to see. The hype in L.A. showed me the pictures and gave me the names: New York, New York; Venetian; Bellagio; Luxor; Aladdin; Paris; Capri; and the rest of the newcomers where once Caesar's Palace had reigned supreme. But now I was here, driving past them at ten o'clock at night, people all over the sidewalks and cars jamming both sides of the strip, neon signs lighting the way and fighting each other for my attention by announcing the name of each hotel and the stars on display that night, fountains in the air dancing to the music, volcanoes exploding, laser beams piercing the night sky, action, action, action everywhere. Sin City. Vegas!

The Barbary Coast, according to Mary, was close to the lagoon and cheaper than the other hotels on the strip, and the doorman looked approvingly at the big red Mercedes with the California plates as I wheeled it up to the entrance. His expression changed when I popped the trunk and he saw the solitary duffel bag which was my luggage.

"Will you be staying with us?" he asked.

"For a couple of days," I replied. "I'm on my way back to L.A. from a hunting trip in Montana and I thought I'd catch some action. Are the tables friendly?"

"Best on the strip, sir," and he smiled as I tipped him. "I'll have your bags, I mean bag, brought right in and your car will be in the garage. Enjoy your stay."

He handed me a claim check for the car and I walked into the lobby, taking it all in, the people, the lights, the endless rows of gaming tables, the slots marching in formation in a corner of the room, the sound of a jackpot siren going off, a lounge act competing for attention, waitresses with trays of drinks, a craps table where a big winner was surrounded by a crowd three deep cheering him on. I was home, and the urge

63

to be a part of it all came over me as strongly as the craving for a drink. I can't do it, I told myself, this is strictly business, I've got a job to do then get the hell out of here and back to Mary. I checked in and waited for the elevator next to a bank of slot machines strategically placed to give you something to do. Never let them rest, that was Vegas, keep them gambling wherever they were. I wondered if there were slots in the john.

It was still early, Vegas time, and I showered after the long drive and then headed for the lagoon at the Treasure Island. There was a huge crowd waiting for the next free show and I joined it, trying to work my way up to the spot where Mary had tossed the bag into the water, but without much luck because the battle was about to start and the crew was on the deck of the pirate ship, trying to look as if they didn't know what was coming next. The lagoon was quite large and on the side opposite the pirate ship an English man o' war came from behind a point of land and started firing its cannons at the pirates, who jumped into action and returned the fire. The battle was loud and with lots of action, cannons smoking and masts being hit by cannon balls and falling to the deck, until at last the pirates were defeated and the battle was over, a good show considering the price.

The crowd left and I made my way to the third vertical pipe supporting the railing around the lagoon. I peered into the water, black as pitch about six feet below me, and tried to picture Mary running out of the casino with the crowd and throwing the bag full of money into the lagoon; then I went over my plan of attack. I was right about the pirate ship, it was bound to have security of some kind and I couldn't use it as a point of entry into the lagoon, but I could slip in at the corner of the lagoon by knotted rope and leave the same way without making a big splash and it wasn't too far from the money bag, so that checked out.

A man stopped at the railing a few feet from me and leaned way over the rail, looking into the dark water. What's he looking for, what if Mary told someone else about the hidden treasure of Treasure Island, and I stopped breathing, waiting for his next move. It came suddenly, starting with a groan, as he puked his guts into the lagoon and I realized he was drunk and going through a maneuver I had performed many times. I should have felt sorry for him but I didn't. He was throwing up in my swimming pool of the next evening and it made me think about all the others there must have been before him and the thousands of cigarettes, cigars and God knows what else that lay waiting for me in those dark and murky waters. I had seen enough of the lagoon, the plan would work, that was all I wanted to know, and I wanted to get away from there and not look at it again until I had to. There were lots of other sights to see.

I started walking down the strip, taking it all in and checking out each hotel I passed, the Mirage with its white tigers and volcano, Caesar's Palace and the Forum, the Bellagio in all its luxury, the Monte Carlo, New York, New York, with a roller coaster outside and its casino in the middle of Mott Street, and when I looked at my watch it was two a.m. and I had only done part of one side of the street. I caught a cab back to the Treasure Island to see if the sidewalk traffic was gone by that time of night and if I would have the lagoon to myself when I went for my swim. There were still people on the sidewalk all the way down the strip to the lagoon, although not very many, and it looked like I would be lucky to get in and out without becoming another tourist attraction. I added an hour to my projected splashdown, making it 3 a.m., and walked across the street and back to the Barbary Coast to get some sleep.

I looked out the window of my room at the strip below. It was now almost three a.m. and there were people everywhere. Frank Sinatra had it all wrong. New York was not the city that never sleeps, Vegas was. He should have known better. He spent enough time here. I closed the drapes and hit the sack. Ah, a comfortable mattress. Mary was right. It was a nice hotel and the price was right. I didn't know about the tables, they must make their money somewhere. I thought about getting back up and trying my luck but I was asleep before the thought was finished.

chapter seven

Thursday I slept late, had some breakfast, then got the car out of hock and did my shopping for the events of the evening. I laid my purchases out on the bed in the room and went over the plan again, knotting the rope I would climb in and out on, weighting the net bag and the white rope I would use to pull it out, and tying the fish line to one end of the white rope and the other end of the rope to the bag. I adjusted the face mask until it was comfortable and tried the waterproof flashlight for the twelfth time. It was only five o'clock, I had at least three or four hours to wait, and I hate waiting. I'm okay when the action starts but waiting makes me nervous, and when I get nervous I want a drink. I tried lying down on the bed but I couldn't nap so I went over the plan again in my mind. I would get to the lagoon before the battle and take a spot next to the third upright of the railing, then pretend to tie my shoe while I tied the fish line to the upright. During the battle, while everyone was looking at the fight, I would kick the bag over the side and let it and the rope sink, with the other end of the fish line attached to the rope. Then later I would...

I woke with a start. It was dark outside and I groped for the light. It was ten o'clock and there was maybe only one more show left at Treasure Island. I grabbed everything and ran to the elevator. When I got to the lagoon the battle was ending and I thanked my lucky stars for waking me. I took my place at the railing as the crowd left and bent over as if to tie my shoe but instead tied the fish line to the upright; then I stood and stared at the water, recalling the drunk last night, as the crowd slowly gathered for the next battle. There was a huge crowd when the fight finally got under way but I refused to be jostled from my spot at the rail. A mother, father and three kids were next to me, the kids wide-eyed at the roaring of the cannons and the battle taking place before their eyes, and the mother and father having a fight of their own about the $200 limit they had given each other to gamble with and the fact that Dad was already in over $600. I got to watch two battles instead of one, but I knew already the pirates were going to lose their battle and the father was going to lose his.

At the height of the battle between the frigates, when all eyes were on the fight, I nudged the bag over the side and watched it fall, then stop in mid-air, half way between the water and the sidewalk, caught in the fish line I must have tangled in my rush to get here. I stood there frozen, not knowing what to do, when one of the kids next to me, a boy about eight, pointed to the bag suspended in mid-air and said, "Look, Mommy, magic." Mom paid no attention to him because she was winning the fight and she wanted to press for an unconditional surrender, but the kid had my attention and I told him it wasn't magic and showed him the fish line to quiet him up.

"What are you fishing for?" he asked.

"Crabs," I replied, remembering my days as a kid on the

Santa Monica pier, "they crawl into the bag."

The fight next to me had grown quiet.

"Don't talk to strangers, Bobby," Mommy said.

Dad, having gotten his tail kicked for gambling away the rent money, was anxious to redeem himself in front of the wife and kids and pushed me on the shoulder.

"Get lost, creep, before I call the cops. What did you say to my kid about crabbies?"

"Crabs, Dad," Bobby said. "He said he's fishing for crabs and that they crawl into that bag."

They all looked over the edge at the sports bag suspended in mid-air about three feet above the water, then looked back at me.

"Is that what you're doing, fishing for crabs in that water with that bag?" Dad asked incredulously.

"That's what I'm doing," I answered, wanting to get this over with as soon as possible because the battle was ending.

The wife opened her purse and handed me a dollar.

"You poor man," she said, and then turned to the kids. "Come along, children, leave the man alone. George, make the children get away from him."

The kids didn't want to leave the naval battle and you could hear them screaming as they were led away from the crab fisherman. People started to turn away from the lagoon to see what this new excitement was all about and I had to do something with the magical sports bag in a hurry, so I broke the line and let it fall into the drink with the plans I had made so carefully. Then my luck changed, just like that, the way luck does in Las Vegas. There was a flash of desert lightning and a crash of thunder that sounded like it was right on top of us and the skies opened up. Rain is one thing no one expects in Vegas and no one is prepared for it. The crowd melted away in the rain as people ran for the casinos, and the streets were empty as quickly as the rain had come. I had the lagoon to myself at last and

I ran back to my hotel, leaving the lagoon looking forlorn in the rain.

I threw the mask and flashlight into the duffel bag along with the knotted rope, pulled on my sweats and sneakers, and ran back to the lagoon as fast as I could. It was still raining heavily but you can never tell with a desert storm. I tied the rope around the third post, to hell with swimming over from the corner of the lagoon in that water, and let myself down, taking the duffel bag with me. The water wasn't that deep and I could touch the bottom, so I pulled on the mask and dove. I saw the white rope and sports bag immediately but not the money bag. There was a lot of junk on the bottom, as I had known there would be, and I dug around in it but found nothing. I figured the bag might have drifted from its original location and moved my search out from the location of the sports bag, which I figured was ground zero, in concentric half circles from the wall. I got out to about twenty feet from the wall and still there was nothing and I was starting to panic. There was no current and it didn't seem likely that the bag would have drifted this far. Maybe the lagoon had been drained and cleaned and there was a rich pool cleaner sipping daiquiris someplace. More power to him, I didn't want the money in the first place.

I told myself I would give the search up if the rain stopped but it was still pouring so I decided on something new. I would swim along the wall to the post next past the third post and to the post next before the third post on the chance that Mary had made a mistake counting because of the excitement and the pressure she was under. I tried the fourth post and found nothing, so I swam back to the third post and on to the second post. Bingo. There was the money bag, a little the worse for wear, but completely recognizable. I didn't want it to break and spill bundled money all over the floor of the lagoon so I swam back and got the duffel bag and very carefully lifted the money bag into it. I closed the duffel bag and swam back to the rope and climbed out, pulling the rope out after me and tossing it into the duffel bag too. I left the sports bag on the floor of the lagoon as a present for the pool cleaner. It wasn't as good as $300,000 but it was a nice bag.

It was still pouring and I fit right in, dripping wet in my sweats and with my wet duffel bag. The doorman looked at me and said, "You really got soaked. I've never seen it rain so hard."

"Remember *Singing in the Rain*? Wasn't that a great picture?" I asked him.

"Sure was," he answered, looking at me kind of funny. Maybe he had heard about the crab fisherman.

I was in the shower, washing my hair for the third time, when I remembered out of the blue a story I had read a long time ago about this baseball player, a great hitter, who would look around on the ground before every game for hairpins. If he found one that meant he would hit well that day and if he didn't he would strike out. This was a long time before psychiatrists and psychologists and their double-speak arrived on the scene and today they would call it the power of positive or negative thinking, something like that, and the players call it being "in the zone."

The mother and father fighting over their $200 limit were bound to lose before they started because that's what they thought was going to happen. Anyway, it made me think about the rain, that when I saw it I knew right away what to do and I knew it was going to work, and I also knew right now, standing in the shower with shampoo running down my face and into my eyes, that as long as it rained I was in the zone and lady luck was my escort. I turned off the shower, toweled myself off quickly, threw on some clean clothes, and went to the money bag to make a withdrawal.

Sure, I had promised Mary that we would open the bag

together, but this was an emergency, the rain wouldn't last forever, and she would understand. I laid the bag on the bed, still dripping wet, and set about opening it. It was canvas, with a leather top and handle and a small lock closing the leather flap. The lock was badly rusted and corroded and I pried it open with a letter opener without much trouble. I was in a hurry to get downstairs before the rain stopped so I just reached in the bag and pulled out a bundle of wet money, which I put between two towels to dry it out as best I could. It was mostly $100 bills and I counted out $5,000, the amount of my withdrawal, and stuffed the rest back in the bag. I figured I would replace the $5,000 from my winnings, plus something extra for the loan, do a count of the money in the bag, and Mary would just have to take my word that I hadn't skimmed anything. What I won was going toward the little house with the white picket fence anyway, so what difference did it make?

I was in such a hurry to get to the action I actually got out the door and was headed for the elevators before I thought about the bag full of wet money on the bed. When my possessions consisted of a duffel bag full of old clothes and some shaving stuff I didn't have to worry about thieves and burglars, they could take what they wanted, what did I care, but now I was a member of the moneyed class and I had to start thinking that way. I went back to the room and put the bag in the safe in the closet, threw the wet towels in the tub, and looked around the room for any stray money that might have fallen on the floor. No money, but there was a man's pinky ring with a diamond the size of Gibraltar on the floor. I picked it up and looked at it, wondering if it had come from the bag or had been lost by the person who had the room before me, then threw it in the safe with the bag and headed for the tables.

When I got downstairs I checked to make sure it was still raining, and when I saw that it was I turned the $5,000 into chips and headed for the craps tables. Craps has always been my favorite game because I love action and that's where it's at. Baccarat is for snobs who want to be seen behind the velvet rope, and roulette is boring, you put your money on a number and watch the wheel go round, big deal. With craps the bets are all over the table, for or against the shooter, the numbers, the hard ways, a million ways to win or lose in a hurry, and that's what I wanted, lots of action while the rain lasted.

I picked out a table that wasn't busy because I wanted to get hold of the dice as soon as I could and put a $100 chip on the pass line, with the shooter, to test out my theory about the rain. He rolled a seven, so my theory worked, but now I wanted the dice. I could have moved to "Don't Pass" but I hate people who bet against the shooter, it's like calling him a loser, so I put the $200 on the hard eight. That's what he threw, and I picked up the chips, knowing this was going to be a hell of a night for me as long as it rained, and moved my action to the numbers. By the time the dice got around to me I was already up over $4,000.

I picked up the dice and looked at them, getting acquainted, letting them feel the contours of my hand, and put $1,000 on the pass line and $1,000 on eleven, and that's what I rolled. There was a big yell from the other gamblers and the pit boss looked over, but with no great concern, some guy got lucky, so what, the odds would take care of him. I let my winnings on the pass line ride and rolled a four, a tough point, but that didn't bother me, lady luck was sitting beside me, rubbing my thigh, making me hot, and I was hot.

I covered the numbers with all the chips that I had and started an amazing roll, hitting every number but four and seven, on and on and on, all the people at the table going crazy and others coming to see what the excitement was all about, money rolling in on my bets, and then a four after about fifteen throws of the dice. The crowd let out a big cheer and I tossed some chips to the guys working the table as I pulled in my winnings and picked up the dice that were offered to me, savoring the moment, in control, all eyes on me waiting to see what I would do. The pit boss was watching me now and talking with the crew, what in hell was I doing, where was I cheating, and I'm sure the eye in the sky was on me too, but I wasn't cheating, I was on a roll, I was in the zone, and there was nothing they could do. I pushed most of my chips on the pass line and looked at the pit boss as they spilled over in an untidy mess and he reached forward to straighten them, catching his eye and holding it as I shook the dice in my hand, waiting, waiting, and then throwing them the length of the table. Seven!

They changed the crew, they changed the dice, they looked at the dice I was using after each roll to make sure I wasn't switching them, they offered me free booze to get me high, they tried everything in the book, but I wasn't cheating so nothing worked, I was killing them and they couldn't do a thing about it. When I finally lost the dice I was up somewhere over $100,000, I didn't have time to count, and I put $1,000 on the pass line to see if lady luck was just fooling around or if she really had left me. The next shooter crapped out and it was time to see if it was still raining outside, so I picked up my chips and headed for an exit.

The strip was underwater and traffic was a mess but the rain had stopped and the moon was shining down on the scene, so it was time for me to quit. I cashed in $127,000 and change in chips and asked the cashier to set up an account for me and give me $10,000 in cash, which was for the bag up in the room. The house was so grateful that I was leaving the money there, meaning to them that I would gamble there again and give them a chance to get it back, that they offered a complimentary suite on the top floor complete with fruit basket and champagne. I declined politely because I had no plans to gamble there again, unless it rained, and I had already taken them for plenty, so why rub it in. A few hours ago I had checked in with a duffel bag full of old clothes and a credit card and now I had an account with $117,000 in it and a pocketful of money. They didn't have to give me a free room, I already loved the place.

 It was past two o'clock and I should have been tired when I got back to my room but I wasn't. I wanted to call Mary and tell her about the night but I couldn't because there would be a record of the call, so I pulled the moneybag out of the safe to take inventory and add the $10,000 I had in my pocket. This time I put towels on the floor instead of using the bed and dumped the contents of the bag onto the towels. There was still water in the bag and it spilled out onto the floor along with wads of wet money, a lot of jewelry that looked like the real McCoy, and something wrapped in a hotel laundry bag from the Capri with scotch tape all over it. The whole pile on the floor looked more like a haul from a burglary than money scooped up in a hurry from the cashiers' cage at the Treasure Island, and I picked up a couple of pieces of jewelry and looked at them closely. They were real, as far as I could tell, and worth a lot of money, and while they could have been pledged as collateral for a loan to a gambler down on his luck, it was unlikely they would be left in the cashiers' cage instead of a safe in the hotel. I counted out the money and it came to $247,000 before I added the $10,000 to it.

 I picked up the package, starting to get a queasy feeling in my stomach, and tore off the plastic laundry bag wrapping and scotch tape, which must have been intended to protect the contents from the water but didn't do a very good job, and was left with what looked like an account book with a gray canvas cover. I opened the book to page after page of handwritten figures, some quite clear and some largely obliterated by the water, interrupted now and then by a total, a distribution to a bunch of names, a date and someone's handwritten initials, maybe "T.D.," maybe not. The dates went back ten years or more and the totals, by quick scan, came to fifty or sixty million dollars. What to make of it I didn't know, but I did know, beyond any doubt, that a robber would not pick up this book even if it was in the cashiers' cage and wrap it in a plastic bag and scotch tape before taking it with him. It was wrapped, maybe in a hurry, by someone who planned on throwing it in the lagoon, and that someone was probably Mary. The sick feeling hit me full force and I fought back the nausea as I saw, quite clearly in my mind's eye, the white picket fence in ashes in front of the little house in Virginia City, Montana.

Sleep was out of the question and I pulled my clothes back on again, put some cash in my pocket, and threw the whole mess, the rest of the money, the jewelry, the towels, the torn laundry bag, everything, back into the bag and into the safe, then headed for the Treasure Island casino. The strip was still flooded but I sloshed across the street anyway, not giving a damn about wet feet, knowing that Las Vegas never shuts down and that there would be gambling and gamblers in the casino. I picked out a blackjack table with a woman dealer and sat down, waiting for the hand to finish. There were only a few people at the table and the hand went quickly, as blackjack does, and I got in the game. I bet the minimum every time, not caring whether I won or lost, just waiting for the others at the table to leave, so I could strike up a conversation with the dealer.

It was now very late and it wasn't long before I was the only one at the table. I tried to sound lonely and friendly, but not on the make, as I asked her the question she must hear over and over every night of every year. "How long have you been dealing blackjack at the Treasure Island?"

She looked tired and answered listlessly, "About five years. It's a job."

She had to have known Mary, and I said, "I have a friend that used to deal blackjack here until a few months ago, you probably know her."

"Probably do," she replied without interest, "what's her name?"

"Mary Carter," I answered.

" 'Fraid not," she said without raising her eyes from the cards, "she must have worked at another casino."

"No, she said it was the Treasure Island," I told her, putting out another bet to keep her talking to me. "Can I describe her to you and maybe you'll remember her?"

She nodded and when I was finished she said, "She sounds like a real looker. I would have remembered her if she was a dealer here. Maybe she was putting you on."

"What about the robbery, do you remember that?" I asked her desperately, putting out another bet.

"What robbery?" she wanted to know.

"About five or six months ago, three guys tried to stick up the cashier right here in the casino. They grabbed some money bags but were shot and killed before they got outside. You must remember that."

"I sure would if it happened, but I think your lady friend was smoking something the night she told you that. There's never been a try at a robbery as long as I've worked here, or since the place was built so far as I know," she said, then looked at me and added sadly, "She really got to you, huh?"

"In more ways than one," I agreed, then tipped her and said good night.

I walked back to the hotel in a daze. What the hell was going on? Why would she make up a story like that? She wanted me to get the bag out of the lagoon for her, that was clear, and she must have known what was in the bag, so why didn't she just say that there was a bag with a lot of money and jewelry in it and she needed my help in pulling it out of the lagoon? If there was no robbery she wasn't wanted by the police, so why couldn't she come with me to Las Vegas? She seemed genuinely terrified of returning here.

I laughed at myself. "Genuinely terrified," I said out loud, "bullshit." There wasn't anything genuine about her from day one so far as I could tell, and I got conned into coming to Las Vegas to do her dirty work, that was for sure, but now I had a bag full of money and jewelry and her car and I could take off and have the last laugh if I wanted. But did I want to? I knew the answer to that. She could have the money and jewelry, no questions asked, if she told me that she loved me and meant it, but I could never trust her again, that was what was sad and tore me up. I went up to my room and looked out the window at the big moon that now filled the sky, and fell asleep in my chair.

chapter eight

    I woke when the morning sun hit my eyes and I showered and shaved, trying to figure out what to do, until at last I decided that I should at least double check with the police before taking the answers of the blackjack dealer of the night before at face value. The problem was that I didn't know what to ask. Something happened about five or six months ago that made Mary throw the bag in the lagoon and skip town, I would take that as a given, and it probably happened at the Capri and in a hurry because she used a laundry bag from the hotel to wrap the book, not exactly what you would choose if you had more time. Had she broken into a room to steal the money and jewelry? But then why did she take the account book that was worth nothing, and go to the trouble of wrapping it? Maybe it was a robbery, like she said, only she changed the location from the Capri to the Treasure Island, but she was like no robber I ever saw before, it didn't fit her profile.

    I would have to be very careful talking to the police because I might become the prime suspect in whatever crime had been committed, the criminal returning to the scene of the crime in search of the missing loot, the plot of a hundred movies.

That's how the idea hit me, the plot of a hundred movies, a retired cop, a rogue cop, a crooked cop, it didn't make any difference, who has left the force and become a private eye, is hired by an insurance company, it didn't make any difference which one, to find the missing jewelry, painting, bonds, whatever. I would flash my badge and explain that I was now retired and trying to make a buck, a sympathetic situation to a cop facing life on a pension someday, and that I couldn't divulge my client, or very much other info, because it was confidential.

Since I didn't really know what I was investigating, a burglary, a robbery, something else, I would call it a "caper," a phony, phony word used only by private eyes in the movies, if I could get it out without gagging, and the cop I was talking to would probably buy it since I was from L.A., and people talk like that there. Before I saw the cops, however, I needed to check out the Capri, where I figured the "caper" actually took place, to see if anyone there remembered anything that would help me with my "cover," another word used only by private eyes in bad movies. I pulled on sneakers and black socks to go with a pair of yellow shorts, and my brightest shirt, my "cover" as a tourist, and headed across the strip for the Capri. I was getting good at this.

It had been built ten or more years ago, at the start of the building boom in Vegas, and was the queen of the strip before the Venetian and the Bellagio came along. It was spectacular still. While most of the theme hotels had gone for miniaturization, a smaller Statue of Liberty or Eiffel Tower, the Capri had gone the other way. Its theme was the Blue Grotto and it had been built on a scale of one hundred feet of the Las Vegas grotto for every one foot of the real grotto to allow room for restaurants and shops along its banks. It opened onto a huge outdoor pool, of course, with a swim-up bar inside the grotto, and if you were dressed there were gondolas on a track to take you from the outside to the dock of the restaurant of your choice or the wedding chapel. The blue light was created by electricity, not by Mother Nature, and changed on a timer to violet, green and orange.

It was only ten in the morning and the casino was mostly empty, with only a few tables open. I found a woman blackjack dealer without anyone at her table and said good morning as I sat down. She gave me a friendly hello, it was morning and she wasn't yet worn out and exhausted like the dealer of last night, and we started playing. There wasn't much for her to keep track of, or watch out for, since I was the only player at her table, and it was easy to make small talk with her. She had been at the Capri for two years and I asked if she knew Mary Carter who used to deal blackjack here, and described her when she said that she didn't. The description didn't help her memory so I changed the subject.

"Were you on duty when they had the shooting here about six months ago?" I asked, adding that it must have been scary. I didn't call it a robbery or a burglary, that was too specific, just a shooting, acting like I knew all about it.

"Yeah," she replied, "but I didn't find out about it till later. It was up in Big Tony's suite, so we didn't hear a thing down here." She paused, thinking about it, and I held my breath.

"I never would have thought Marc would do a thing like that, he seemed like such a nice boy."

Who the hell was Marc, I asked myself, and chose my next question carefully. "Did you know him well?"

"He was one of the lifeguards at the pool," she answered, "so I didn't see a lot of him, but he was such a good-looking kid, even at my age you kind of notice, if you know what I mean, and so friendly, like you." She gave me a get-together-later kind of smile and I knew I was in.

"What do you mean, your age," I replied, "you must be all of thirty." She was about forty-five but you can never guess a woman's age too young, only too old.

"I wish," she flustered. "He was so young, about twenty-five, and he had to beat the women at the pool away from him with a stick he was so handsome, he had everything to live for, why would he do a stupid thing like sticking up Big Tony?"

It was the second time she had mentioned Big Tony, and I didn't have a clue who he was, so I had to ask, "Who is Big Tony? I'm from out of town."

"Oh, I forgot, everyone in Vegas knows who Big Tony is: Tony Danzante. He owns this place although that isn't what the deed says, he built it with money from back east. He's from Jersey but he lives out here, if you can call it living the way he is now."

Tony Danzante, "T.D.," I thought, and asked, "What's the matter with him?"

"He was shot by one of the robbers, maybe Marc, he's a paraplegic now from the waist down. I had to have it explained to me, he can't even go to the bathroom by himself." She grimaced. "Isn't that awful?"

I saw my opening and asked, "What happened to the other robbers?"

"There was only one other, according to Big Tony, and he's never been caught, but most people think that Big Tony's had him taken care of by now, he's a guy you don't mess with. It was really dumb to try to stick him up."

It was getting busy and another player sat down at the table, stopping the conversation. I cursed him under my breath, there were so many more questions I wanted to ask, and played quietly until he lost about fifty bucks and had enough.

When he left the table I pushed out a hundred dollar bet and said, "I'm in town all by myself and I haven't been to Vegas in about fifteen years. Where's a good place to have dinner?"

"I like Canaletto at the Venetian," she said and smiled. "It's got a nice outdoor eating area, or at least it seems like it's outdoors, the food is good and it's not expensive."

"If you don't have other plans for tonight I'd really like you to have dinner with me. My name's Mike Driscoll, by the way." I smiled.

"Hi, I'm Sally Paquette," she smiled back, "and we're not supposed to date customers, especially if we steer them to another hotel, but I'd love to. I'm sick of the Blue Grotto."

We kept playing blackjack while she continued on. "I get off my shift at four and I want to go home and freshen up, so I'll meet you in front of the restaurant at seven, if that's okay."

"Perfect," I said, as two players started to sit down at her table. "I'll see you then, Sally."

chapter nine

Any police station is pretty much the same in any city, some are newer and some are older, but they all have graffiti in the john, there are cops and perps coming and going, they're noisy and smelly, the furniture is cheap, and the help have watched too much TV and act and talk like *N.Y.P.D. Blue* and *Law and Order*. Detective Bill Accardo handed me back my badge and looked at me over his plastic and chrome desk.

"So how's retirement?" he asked.

"Not what it's cracked up to be," I answered. "Someone fills your place as soon as you're gone and you're an outsider, trying to make it on a pension, looking for something to do. Hang on as long as you can and make them throw you out, Bill."

He laughed but the answer caught him by surprise, and I could see he felt sorry for me and that was the way I wanted him.

"What can I do for you, Mike?" he asked, and we were on a first-name basis.

"I'd like to take a look at the file on the Tony Danzante robbery about six months ago," I said, using the information I had picked up from Sally in the morning.

"Who are you working for?" he asked.

"The insurance company," I replied. "It's my first assignment from them and I want to do a real good job. This is a big break for me, just starting out and all."

"Why are they interested? All they paid for was $10,000 in the safe and Tony's pinky ring. They declined the claim on the jewelry and didn't pay a dime on it, is what I hear. The jewelry didn't belong to Big Tony, it belonged to the broad, and no one can find her, she's never made a claim."

Mary, I thought, and tried to figure out a way to answer his question. I had to wing it.

"They're worried about a bad faith claim because they didn't pay on the jewelry and they want to back up the reasons for their refusal in case they're sued," I said and crossed my fingers.

"I guess I can let you see it," he said. "The case is closed now anyway."

It was my turn to ask a question. "Why is the file closed? There were two robbers, I was told, and one has never been caught."

"Never will be either," Bill answered. "The word was passed down from a friend of a friend of a friend, hearsay in other words, that Big Tony said to close the file because he would take care of the other guy. He's probably out in the desert now pushing up cactus. He would have been better off if we had picked him up."

"What about the jewelry that was stolen? That's what my client is interested in. Aren't you still looking for that?"

"Why?" he asked, looking at me like I was slow and he could understand why I had never made detective.

I guess I am slow, because I didn't get it, and I asked,

"Why not?"

Bill looked at me condescendingly and said, "There were two perps, right, one was killed and the other one got away with the goods, right, then Big Tony finds the one that got away and kills him, but before he kills him do you think he didn't ask where the goods were, that's not Big Tony, he would have cut him apart inch by inch until the guy spilled his guts, then he would have killed him, and that's why we closed the file."

"So you think Big Tony has everything back that was taken?" I asked, feeling like Sam Spade as I rolled Big Tony off my tongue.

"That's our theory," Bill replied, "but don't quote me to the insurance company on that, that's strictly off the record."

"Then I guess I'll have to go through the file and draw my own conclusions," I said. "Can I have a room for an hour or two?"

"Sure," Bill answered, friendly now that he had explained everything to the poor dim wit in front of him, and feeling sorry for me in my new career as a private eye, in which I'm sure he felt I was bound to fail. He got the file, took me to an empty interrogation room, and closed the door.

The robbery took place in the penthouse suite of the Capri, which had been occupied by Tony and his live-in girlfriend, Theresa Defoe, since the hotel opened. The police had been called when the maid came in to make up the room and found Tony and Marc Gambino apparently dead on the floor. The paramedics pronounced Gambino dead at the scene of two gunshot wounds in the chest but Tony was still alive and was rushed to the hospital, where he was in a coma for ten days and woke up a paraplegic from the waist down with a bullet in his spine. He gave a statement to the police that he had returned from a business trip to New Jersey and entered the suite about ten in the morning. He didn't notice anything wrong at first but when he went to the bedroom he found two men working on the safe that was in the closet. One was Marc Gambino, whom he recognized as a lifeguard at the pool, and the other was a tall black man about forty years old that he did not know.

The two men saw him, drew their guns and forced him to open the safe. While they were putting the contents of the safe into a canvas bag the black man put down his gun, which Tony grabbed in an attempt to stop them, and there was a gunfight between him and the younger man, Marc Gambino. He didn't know whether he had hit Gambino, but he was hit and the next thing he remembered was waking up in the hospital. He described the contents of the safe as jewelry valued at $500,000 and about $10,000 in cash that he kept on hand. There was no mention of the $250,000 that I had found in the bag or the account book. His trademark diamond pinky ring was also missing and he presumed the black man had taken it off his finger before he left. He gave his age as seventy-one.

Theresa Defoe had returned to the suite about four p.m. and found the police there. She stated that she had left about nine a.m. and had spent the day shopping. Nothing was amiss when she left and she did not notice anyone in the hall. She had visited the shops at the Forum, the Bellagio and the Aladdin and had lunch at the Bellagio. She gave her age as thirty-six. Her statement had been checked out and verified. She had excused herself from the interview shortly after arriving at the suite to be with Tony and had been with him every day at the hospital until his family arrived from New Jersey. Tony denied any knowledge of her whereabouts and filed a missing persons report but she had not been found. There was a photograph of her on the missing persons report and it was Mary but her hair in the picture was black as a crow. An intensive search was made for the black man but it was ten days late because of Tony's coma and the description was vague. He was not found and there were no other suspects.

I skipped to the forensics portion of the file. There was an X-ray report that Tony had a bullet lodged in his spine and an autopsy report on Gambino. Tony must be a hell of a shot. Gambino had taken two slugs to the heart, the entry wounds only millimeters apart, and had died instantly. The bullets were examined and came from the gun found in Tony's hand. Both guns were .38's but had their serial numbers filed off and were untraceable. Tony was dressed in a suit, shirt and tie, consistent with his statement that he was returning from a business trip to New Jersey, and Gambino was dressed for Las Vegas in a silk sport shirt, slacks and loafers without socks. He was not wearing any undershirt or pants but had a gold chain around his neck. There were powder burns on Gambino's sport shirt, indicating he was shot at close range, but no powder burns on Tony's suit. It was theorized that Gambino shot first and that Tony fell forward, shooting on the way down, and possibly grabbing Gambino as he fell.

I closed the file and sat there, thinking about what I had just read. Who was the black man and how did he fit in? Why had Tony only reported $10,000 as missing when I had found $250,000 in the bag? Was Mary a third accomplice with Marc and the black man and, if so, why would she steal her own jewelry and then disappear instead of making an insurance claim, if that was the scam? My head hurt. I was just a cop, not a detective, and I had only questions, no answers. I returned the file to Bill, thanked him and left the police station.

I had a lot of time on my hands before seven o'clock so I went to the local newspaper and asked to see their clippings files on Tony Danzante and Theresa Defoe. They were on microfilm, naturally, not like the old days, and I was shown into a room and checked out on how to operate the machine before I was left alone. There was not much on Mary, or Theresa, or whatever the hell her name was, which didn't surprise me.

THE CAPO'S MISTRESS

There were pictures of her at various functions, charity fund raisers, society balls, and the like, looking beautiful in evening gowns that must have cost a fortune, decked out in her finest jewelry, all in the company of Tony. The caption on one photo said she was from Palm Beach, or as the caption put it, "of Palm Beach, Florida," and I wondered what had happened to Bisbee, Arizona. It made me think of Jackie Kennedy and Aristotle Onassis, the princess and the frog, only a kiss wouldn't turn either Ari or Tony into Prince Charming. I don't know what Jackie saw in Ari, she had lots of money of her own, but Mary was out for the good life, that was for sure, and I wondered if she had been happy then.

Tony was another matter and his file was thick and took a lot of reading. When the Capri was being built he had applied for a gambling license and was turned down because of his mob connections. His father was Piero Danzante, the head of the New Jersey crime family in the twenties and thirties, and a notorious bootlegger who had emigrated from Naples. When his father died it was speculated, but never proved, that Tony became the head of the family, the capo, and he had been arrested several times on drug charges but never convicted. He came into his own when gambling was legalized in Jersey and there was testimony at the hearing on his license application for the Capri that he controlled all of the gambling in Atlantic City and you couldn't do business there without a kickback to Tony in one form or another. His application for a gambling license in Nevada was denied and the guy who testified against him at the hearing later had his car go over a bridge railing in New Jersey and was killed. He had a blood alcohol reading of .27 and the crash was found to be accidental. After testimony that Tony had divested himself of any interest in the Capri a license was given to the new owners of the hotel.

Tony had been married for forty-one years to the same woman and had three children, one boy and two girls. The family lived in New Jersey, which was Tony's legal residence, but he had spent most of his time in Las Vegas since the opening of the Capri, where he had a penthouse suite.

There were rumors that Tony was in Vegas to represent the interests of the investors in the Capri, from whom he had raised most of the money for its construction, and that receipts were down because of competition from the new hotels on the strip. Tony was described as devoted to his family and he made frequent trips back to New Jersey to visit them. His son, Piero, was thirty-three at the time of the article I was reading and was described as "on track" to succeed Tony when he stepped down.

I finally got down to clippings about the robbery and the outpouring of grief when it appeared that Tony would die. He was described as a visionary responsible for the construction of one of the most spectacular hotels on the strip and a pillar of the community who worked tirelessly for charitable causes. There was a picture of Tony leaving Mass with his family on one of their infrequent visits to Las Vegas, and the pastor was quoted as calling him the person most responsible for the building of the church by the generous donation of his time and money to its construction. He was a man of great faith, the pastor went on to say, and he asked the congregation to pray for his recovery. There were no pictures of Mary.

I didn't learn anything more about the robbery than I had gotten from the police file, which was to be expected, and I shut down the machine and ordered a print of Mary wearing an emerald necklace to check against the jewelry I had in the room and then headed for the Barbary Coast mulling it all over. I had a lot more information but I couldn't put the pieces together and I was trying for the umpteenth time to answer the same questions when it hit me: I didn't have to answer the questions, I wasn't the detective on the case, Accardo was, I was just a retired cop and I was on an ego trip playing detective, trying to beat Accardo at his own game. I came here to do a job and I had done it. The question I was trying to dodge with all this detective stuff was what to do with the bag I had pulled out of the lagoon. I could keep it or return it to Mary, I still thought of her by that name, or turn it over to the police. I ruled out keeping it, that would be a double-cross, like ratting on your partner, and I wasn't built that way, so it was between Mary and the cops, but if I turned the bag over to the police I would have to tell them how I got it, the whole thing would unravel, and Mary would be arrested for felony-murder or at least as an accomplice to the black man, who must have given her the bag and was probably waiting for her now in Tahiti.

To hell with it, I can't solve the problems of the world, give her the bag and be done with it. I didn't ever want to see her again because that would make me want to be with her. I still had it bad despite what I had learned, and I knew down deep that she wasn't finished with me and if I brought back the bag there would be more she wanted me to do, and I wouldn't want to do it but I would, just like I had covered up for Five.

I stopped at the Bellagio and walked down the shopping wing, passing the swell shops, Prada, Escada and the rest, thinking of Mary going in and out of them on the day of the robbery to establish an alibi, until I found a fancy gift store. I picked out a big wooden box full of candied fruit, which I have hated since the day as a kid when I ate too many candied cherries and threw up on the living room sofa, but I was buying it for the box, not the contents. I asked them to wrap it as a gift, which they were more than happy to do at a price tag of $250, and when I got back to my room I looked for the emerald necklace Mary was wearing in the print I ordered. It was there, there was no switch going on, and I carefully removed the wrapping on the box, slid back the wooden cover, and dumped all the fruit into the wastebasket. The ledger book and the money were still damp so I wrapped them in a plastic laundry bag along with the jewelry, just like Mary, and put the package in the box. There was room left over and I filled it with candied cherries.

It was time for the letter and I wrote "Dear Mary," then threw that sheet of paper in the wastebasket on top of the fruit and started a new sheet of paper with, "To Mary, Theresa, or whatever the hell your name is," and began the letter. I told her that I loved her and would probably never get over her but that I could never trust her again after what I had found out about her and the story she had given me, and that I never wanted to see her again and would leave her car with Sam when I picked up mine. I said I found the bag and opened it and knew now why she didn't want me to see what was inside. I said all the money was in the box, although I was sure if our places were switched she would keep the money and skip, then I told her about borrowing the $5,000 to gamble, how much I had won, and that I had replaced the $5,000 and added $5,000 to it for the loan, which was something she would never do because she loved money more than anything. I told her I wished with all my heart that we could grow old together in the little house in Virginia City, with a white picket fence I would build and paint, but I knew now that she never intended to live there, that she used that to get me to do her dirty work, and that she had broken my heart. I thought about signing it "Love, Mike," but just wrote Mike, then put the letter in an envelope, put the envelope on top of the bag, and slid the top of the box shut. I re-wrapped the box and took it to the closest Fed Ex office and it was on its way, overnight delivery; Mary would have the bag of money and jewelry on Saturday, as promised, but not me. I didn't want to hang around Virginia City waiting for my car, the temptation to see Mary would be too great, so I figured I would drive back Tuesday and pick up my car that evening, when it was supposed to be ready, then hit the road

THE CAPO'S MISTRESS

for L.A., with a stopover in Helena for the long-overdue A.A. meeting.

chapter ten

It was time to get ready for dinner with Sally but that was a waste of time now, there was nothing I could learn from her that I didn't already know, and I thought about canceling, but it was after four o'clock and that was the end of her shift at the Capri. I tried to find her number in the phone book but she wasn't listed. I couldn't stand her up, that had happened to me a lot when I was a fat slob and I could still remember the hurt, so I started to get dressed, dreading the evening.

I walked down to the Venetian early because I hadn't seen it yet and wanted time to look around. I've never been to Venice, or to Europe for that matter, and I guess the entrance was supposed to represent St. Mark's Square, or at least that's what I thought St. Mark's Square would look like from the pictures I had seen. There was a bridge to go over and you were inside, looking at the casino, nice and handy but nothing to take your breath away, if you've seen one casino you've seen them all, you go there to gamble, not look around, so I went upstairs. That was more like it. The ceiling was high and painted with clouds, lighted so that you would swear you were outdoors, and underneath the sky there was a canal with gondoliers singing in Italian as they poled their passengers along, under bridges which crossed back and forth to shops and restaurants. A wedding was taking place on one of the bridges and there were happy strollers everywhere. I walked along the canal looking into the shops, reading the menus outside the restaurants like any other tourist and looking at the white medieval statues, which were live and would move every now and then to give you a start.

Canaletto was at the end of the canal across a bridge filled with picture-takers and looked out on a large piazza surrounded by shops. It was seven o'clock and I stood at the entrance to a courtyard filled with tables, taking in the scene, waiting for Sally to arrive fashionably late, when I saw her waving to me from a table next to the railing, ringside on the piazza. People were streaming by in back of her and you would swear she was outside at a sidewalk table in Rome or Florence or Milan, not inside a Vegas hotel with air-conditioning.

She stood up to greet me as I joined her and, as the expression goes, she had cleaned up good. She wore a uniform at the Capri and now she was in a filmy dress and had done something with her hair. She looked great and I told her so. She was no Mary, who stopped your breath, but she had something about her, a girl next door quality, that made you look twice.

"I got here early to get a good table, I hope you don't mind," she said, and I thanked her and told her that I didn't mind at all, realizing that she thought we were on a date and was doing her very best to make it work, and I didn't think of it that way at all. I had asked her to dinner to pump her for information and now I had the information and all this was a waste of time. I guess my thoughts showed in my face because she asked, "Did you have a bad day at the tables?"

All right, asshole, I told myself, you didn't want to hurt her feelings by standing her up, so now are you going to pout all evening and make her wish she wasn't here too? She got all dressed up and got here early to find us a good table, so be nice, for Christ's sake. I will, I will, I answered back, but give me a break, can't you see my heart is broken? It's my heart too, you jerk, don't be such a wuss and suck up the pain.

I looked up and saw that Sally was waiting for an answer to her question, a half smile on her face, wondering what was taking all the time. I came out of my trance and smiled back.

"No, as a matter of fact I didn't gamble at all, just looked around the town, it's been a long time since I've been to Vegas."

I fell silent again and she looked around for something to keep the conversation going and then said, "Oh, look, he's leaving." One of the white statues had stepped off the small pilaster on which he was standing and was walking away. Probably has to go to the can, I thought, as a large group of people of all ages came over the bridge, laughing and talking one on top of the other. It looked like they were coming from a birthday party for one of them, and they all stopped in front of the vacant pilaster in the piazza and one of the kids said in a surprised voice, "He's gone." The laughter stopped and another voice said, "Darn," and then this old guy who looked like he was loaded, it must have been the grandpa, climbed up on the pilaster in a suit, shirt and tie and stood there like he was the statue. His wife or daughter, she looked a lot younger than he did, told him that he was drunk and to get down, but he wouldn't, then one of the kids put a dollar bill on the pilaster in front of him and he tried to pick it up, but every time he did the kid would snatch it away just in time and he would stand up again. A crowd started to gather, they thought it was an act, and soon there was money all over the pilaster. Sally and I both couldn't stop laughing and the ice was broken.

"You know, I didn't have lunch today and I'm starved, what's good here?" I asked.

"Everything," she said with enthusiasm, "the food here is wonderful."

As it turned out, I hated to see the dinner end, and when we finished we strolled back along the canal arm in arm and out onto a balcony overlooking the bridge and St. Mark's Square, the pirate ship and lagoon of Treasure Island beyond, and in the distance a full moon over the Mirage. We leaned on the rail, taking it all in, no words necessary any longer, and she turned to me with her eyes closed, expecting to be kissed.

What are you waiting for? I asked myself. Go ahead and kiss her. I'm not ready for this, I answered back, you know where this will lead and I'm not ready, it's too soon. Too soon, what the hell is that supposed to mean, you take it where you find it and you're going to get lucky tonight, don't go dramatic on me, you jerk. You're the jerk, I said back, she's a nice girl, we had a good time tonight, and I'm not going to mislead her, I'm not ready for another relationship and she doesn't know that. You poor, dumb sap, came the answer, you know what she's ready for and you're blowing it.

Sally opened her eyes and looked at me, still close, wondering what was taking so long.

"We've got to talk," I said.

She stepped away. "I know what that means," she said, "you're married."

"No," I replied, "divorced. A long time ago."

"Are you gay?" she asked.

"No," I answered haltingly, "it's just that last Monday I proposed to a girl I thought was wonderful, I was on top of the world, and now it's over and I'm not ready to start a new relationship. I think I'm still in love with her."

"Then why did you ask me to dinner?" she asked slowly

in a puzzled voice, her eyes starting to look wet.

Well, how are you going to answer that, big shot? I asked myself. Are you going to tell her you were using her to get information but now you don't need her anymore and you took her to dinner because you couldn't find her number in the phone book to cancel out? That will make her feel just swell and I'm sure she will think it was very noble of you, you piece of shit.

"I was lonely," I stammered, head down, wishing I could go back to the moment when she was standing there, eyes closed, waiting to be kissed. I thought maybe she would feel sorry for me and let me off the hook, duplicitous bastard that I am, but instead she got mad, no tears, and her eyes flashing now.

"You're lonely, who the hell isn't? This whole goddamn town is lonely. Look around you. Do you think this is Venice? It's an adult Disneyland where everyone is trying to forget their troubles. All I wanted out of this evening was a chance to forget mine for a few hours and live in a dream world again, like when I was growing up and everything was going to be perfect. I didn't want a relationship, if that's what you call it, I'm forty-seven years old and you told me you were from out of town. I knew that would never happen. I just wanted one night with you, was that too much to ask? So I paid fifty dollars to have my hair done, and another ten for my nails, money I couldn't afford, to look as good as I could and get away from my life for a few hours, and now you've ruined it, and it was going so well."

She stopped and now the tears came, buckets of them, and I put my arm around her to comfort her and tried to raise her face to kiss her but she pulled away.

"I don't want a pity kiss," she said. "No thanks."

She ran down the stairs and I let her go.

THE CAPO'S MISTRESS

I walked across the street to the Treasure Island and looked in the lagoon. The girl I was in love with, used to be in love with, whatever, was mixed up in the robbery but not for the cash or the jewelry, that didn't make sense, it was her own jewelry, and the cash wasn't that much compared to what she was risking. It was the book, it had to be the book, and I wanted it back to try to figure what the robbery was all about but it was on its way to Mary. I tried to remember it. Columns of numbers, 50 or 60 million dollars, the initials "TD" for Tony Danzante, and a bunch of names who were getting the money. I had recognized some of them. They were members of the syndicate, like the Gambino family. It was a scam of some kind, maybe tax evasion, and with the book she could blackmail Tony for a lot of money. That was a dangerous game, and she knew it, that was why she was hiding out. Tomorrow she would have the book by Fed Ex but she couldn't blackmail Tony all by herself and that was where I would come in. I was lucky enough to find out about her and now she's on her own. It'll never work. She's as good as dead.

I walked back to the Barbary Coast feeling about as low as I've ever been. It was still early, about eleven o'clock, and I didn't know what to do with myself. All I could think about was what Sally had said and how true it was. I had been living a fantasy, a Disneyland of little houses with white picket fences, and it had come crashing down around me, as fantasies always do.

I wandered around the casino, watching the action, and finally stepped up to the craps table that had been so kind to me, the high roller returning to the scene of his triumph. Why not? I thought. It's not raining, I answered back, you were only going to shoot craps when it's raining, remember? Yeah,

I remember, and I'm not supposed to walk under ladders or let a black cat cross my path either, you superstitious old woman, just gimmie the goddamn dice.

A server appeared as if by magic with a tray of drinks, not to the liking of the high roller, and I asked for a Jack Daniels mist and told her to keep them coming. Later I was able to remember the first eight or nine hours, but nothing after that although they told me I was still on my feet all day Saturday until around seven o'clock, almost twenty hours of continuous craps shooting. I was hot at first and by 3 A.M. I was up over $300,000. The word got around that the same guy was back and was killing the house and people were six deep at the table, trying to see the action. I'm a happy drunk, like I said, and I started throwing $100 chips to the crowd when I won big, the onlookers going crazy trying to grab the free money. The pit boss told me to stop or he would have to call security and I said that I was tired and it was probably time to call it quits anyway and this would be my last roll.

I wish he had the courage of his convictions but he knew that if he could keep me gambling and not let a big winner get away the odds would eventually catch up with me. I knew it too, but by then I was too far gone to remember it, high on the booze, the action and the noise of the crowd when I threw a winner. The pit boss said to hell with security, the crowd let out a big yell, and I couldn't cash out then, they were depending on me, pulling for me, I was their hero, I couldn't let them down.

chapter eleven

I woke up Monday morning feeling awful and did the same thing I had seen the drunk at the lagoon do, only I was hanging over the toilet, not the rail. A nuclear warhead was going off in my head. I took a hot shower for a long time and didn't feel any better so I got dressed and visited the cashier to see how much was in my account, fearing the worst, and I wasn't disappointed. It was all gone and they inquired when I would be checking out. The cashier told me that I had withdrawn the last of my account and started on my credit card around 5 o'clock Saturday afternoon and showed me the signed withdrawal slips to prove it. He said that I had passed out at the table Saturday evening, knocking my remaining chips to the floor, he estimated about $1,000 worth, and that the crowd scooped them up and got away with them before security could be called. I had been taken to my room and put to bed and I had slept all day Sunday. My credit card was maxed out and I looked in my wallet and Lincoln and three Washingtons looked back at me. The high roller was broke and when I told the cashier he called the manager, who thanked me for my patronage and said my run on Saturday brought lots of business through the doors and my room would be comp'd if I left within a reasonable period of time. He shook my hand real friendly like and said that he hoped I had enjoyed my stay.

My money was gone, it once again belonged to the house, God was in His heaven, and all was right with the world. I had a soft-boiled egg in the coffee shop, which I hoped I could keep down, went back up to my room, sat down in my chair, and looked out the window. It was raining. Oh, no, not now, not when I'm broke, why now, God? I waited for a deep voice to say, "There's something about you that pisses me off," but there was no answer.

I went to the safe hoping against hope that a couple of bills fell out of the bag but there was nothing. Then I saw it, way back in the corner where I had thrown it after finding it on the floor. The ring. I pulled it out, knowing now that it was Big Tony's and that the diamond, that impossibly large and garish thing that was sparkling in the light, was real. My head was about to burst and the soft-boiled egg was threatening to appear in front of me again but so what? It was raining and my luck was back, the ring had appeared in my time of need and I was about to break the bank, I could feel it. I swallowed a bunch of aspirin and headed back downstairs.

The cashier looked the ring over and asked, "Where did you get this? You weren't wearing it."

"It was in the safe in my room," I said. "You would have seen it Saturday night if I hadn't passed out. It's worth a lot of money and I need an advance."

The cashier looked hesitant and held the diamond up to the light. "It doesn't look real. It's too big. I'll have to have it appraised."

"How long will that take?" I asked, sounding a little desperate. "I want to get back to the tables, and I mean your tables, not some other casino."

That did the trick. The cashier smiled and said, "I can let you have a thousand dollars while it's being appraised. It's worth at least that much. I'll find you when I get the appraisal and let you know how much more I can advance."

"I won't need any more advances. I don't plan on losing."

Confidence was my middle name, Mike Confidence Driscoll. I said it to myself, it had a nice sound. He counted out the money and looked nervous when I headed for the exit, but I was just checking on the rain, it was coming down hard, and I waved to him as I walked back heading for my favorite craps table.

"Good luck," he mouthed, in the middle of a telephone call.

It was just like before. I put $500 on the pass line and the shooter rolled a seven. I had it back, Lady Luck was beside me again, rubbing my leg, making me hot, and I played the numbers waiting for the dice to come to me, pulling in money at every roll. Finally the dice were mine. I looked at them in the palm of my hand, feeling them, letting them get to know me and like me before I started my roll. I put a couple of thousand on the pass line but as I was about to shoot someone grabbed my arm and a voice said in my ear, "Game's over. Pick up your chips and come with me."

I wheeled, mad as hell to be interrupted now that I had finally gotten the dice, and there was Detective Bill Accardo, a serious look on his face.

"Just pick up your chips and come with me to the cashier's office, please. Don't make me flash my badge."

Oh, God, they've called the cops. Either they've recognized the ring or they think the diamond's a phony, or maybe it is a phony, I don't know, but I've got money to gamble with now, I have to get back to the craps table, how long will it take to straighten this out? I gathered up my chips and walked with Accardo back to the cashier's office. Several people were there but nobody said hello. The cashier cashed me out, deducted the $1,000 advance, and handed me $4,600 in cash.

"Thank you," I said, "where's the ring?"

The cashier nodded at Accardo, who reached in his pocket, put the ring on the table and asked, "Where did you get this, Mike?"

"I won it in a card game." It was pretty lame but it was the best that I could do.

"I might buy that if you hadn't come in last week asking to look at the file on the Danzante robbery and said you were working for the insurance company on the loss, the same insurance company that paid Big Tony off on the ring. Did you have the ring then?"

Oh, oh, I'm in deep shit, I thought, and said, "As a matter of fact I did, but that's not his ring, I won that ring in a card game, like I said."

"Sure looks like Tony's ring to me," Accardo replied. "I guess we'll have to take it over to him and see if he can identify it. In the meantime I'm keeping the ring. You come with me."

As we left the Barbary Coast I noticed it had stopped raining.

chapter twelve

Anthony Danzante, a.k.a. Big Tony, had the penthouse suite at the Capri with a knockout view of the strip far below. When we entered he was in a wheelchair in the living room looking out the floor-to-ceiling window, and he turned the wheelchair to face us but he didn't look anything like the pictures of Big Tony I had seen in the newspaper clippings. That Tony was in his seventies but he was the kind of a guy you would still call Big Tony, larger then life and in charge of everything he surveyed, you could see it in his eyes and the way he carried himself. This Tony still had a big frame but he had shriveled up on it and his robe hung from him. He looked dead until you saw his eyes, which were constantly moving and were small and black and mean. They were not the eyes of the man in the newspaper clippings, he was gone forever.

"Good morning," Accardo said, and nodded to Tony and a couple of tough-looking mugs on a sofa as the man who had let us in went over to the bar. Accardo pulled the ring out of his pocket and handed it to Tony. "Is this your ring?"

Tony put the ring on his little finger and looked at it for a long time until I thought he wasn't going to answer but then he looked up at us and said in a surprisingly loud voice, "Yes. Where is she?"

I didn't answer because I thought he was talking to Accardo and the two mugs got off the sofa and approached us, smiling as they came, until they were right in front of me.

"Mr. Danzante asked you a question, dumb shit," one said without raising his voice, then hit me in the stomach. I wasn't expecting it and neither was the soft-boiled egg, which had always been unsure about settling down there, and out it came, all over the thug's coat.

"Son of a bitch," he screamed, loud now, "that's an Armani suit, you jack off."

He threw a punch at my head, but I was ready now and grabbed his arm as I ducked the punch, rolling him over my hip and onto the floor. Bill grabbed my arms from behind and the other two mugs wrestled me to the floor and held me down while Bill cuffed my hands behind my back. The Armani suit, embarrassed at being thrown to the floor, kicked me in the side to show how tough he was. Things were not going well at all.

Tony rolled his chair up to me and said again, looking at me with his mean little eyes, "Where is she?"

"Who?" I asked, and was slugged by the Armani suit.

"Theresa, you dumb fuck," Tony screamed at me.

"I don't know any Theresa," I answered through a bloody lip. "I saw a missing persons report you filed on a Theresa something or other in the police file, but that's all I know."

"Then where did you get the ring?" Tony asked softly.

"I won it in a card game." That sounded dumb even to me and both mugs slugged me. The other one had gone back to the bar but he came back to get a lick in too.

"Wait a minute, Tony," Accardo said, "let me handle this."

THE CAPO'S MISTRESS

That sounded better to me than the way Tony was handling it and I almost shook my head in agreement.

"You already had the ring when you came in last week and asked to see the file on the Danzante robbery, right?"

"Yes," I answered, knowing where this was going.

"Who were you working for when you came to see me?"

"I told you. The insurance company on the robbery."

"Did you know that the ring you had was taken in the robbery and paid for by the insurance company you say you were working for?"

What do I say, I asked myself, and said, "No, of course not."

"Just a coincidence?"

"It happens," I answered, feeling like a fool.

"What's the name of the insurance company?"

"I told you, that's confidential," I said, knowing that I didn't have a clue what company was on the loss.

Tony broke in, "Bill called the company and they never heard of you, dip shit."

"Let me handle this, Tony," Accardo said in an annoyed voice, and I realized that he had let Tony know about my visit the minute I was out the door and had probably been investigating me since. Ah, well, I thought, another cop on the take, welcome to the club.

"Who are you working for?" Accardo asked.

"That's confidential," I said again.

Accardo nodded to the two mugs and they started in on me. Right in the middle of the beating the phone rang and the mug at the bar picked it up and said, "It's for you, Bill."

"I'll take it in the other room, Lou. Hold everything until I get back." I breathed a sigh of relief and hoped it was a long telephone call. I was left alone with Tony and his three thugs. Tony wheeled his chair over close to me and told the thugs to go into the entrance hall and guard the door in case I tried to get away.

"I don't like to leave you alone with him," the Armani suit said.

"Jesus Christ, Gino," Tony screamed, "don't you think I can handle a guy with his hands cuffed behind him? Get the fuck out of here and get rid of that coat. You smell like puke."

"Sure, boss, sure," Armani whined, "I was just watching out for you like I'm supposed to do."

The three of them left and I was alone with Tony.

"You've slept with her, haven't you?" he asked me, and added, "Don't say who again or I'll have them beat the shit out of you."

That was a hell of an opening line and I tried to figure out what to say, but I didn't have to answer because he kept on talking. "Best piece of ass I ever had, and I've had a lot of them," he continued on. "She never stopped, just kept going and going like that fucking rabbit on TV, all you could do was hang on. Is that the way she was with you?" He smiled at me like we were talking it over in a bar and I almost nodded in agreement, remembering that first night with Mary. It must have shown on my face despite the blood and bruises from the beating because again he didn't wait for my answer and continued on, "Yeah, she was great, wasn't she? Like I said, the best I ever had, and I'll bet she was the best you've ever had too, am I right?"

This was a "Have you stopped beating your wife?" question so I just sat there, waiting for him to continue.

"I'll never be able to do it again," he said. "Look at me, nothing works below my belt, I can't even crap for myself. That god damn pornographer, Larry Flynt, he got what he deserved, but why me? I go to Mass every Sunday rain or shine, I'm heavy in the collection box, I give lots of dough to the poor, I raised money to build the hospital here in Vegas, you name it and I've done it, and look what God gave me in return."

"It must be tough," I ventured.

"Look, I want to see Theresa again, we were together almost ten years," Tony continued. "I don't know why she up and left like she did, maybe it was because she heard I was going to be like this and she couldn't face it, but I still love her and I want her back. Maybe you're in love with her too, you probably are, why wouldn't you be, but I'm willing to make it worth your while to take me to her and step out of the picture."

He paused, this time waiting for me to say something. Was this guy on the level, I asked myself, and answered maybe, but so what, would I turn Mary over to him even if he was? The answer to that was a resounding "NO." Tony was right, despite everything I knew about her I was still in love with Mary and hoped against hope that she was in love with me. Sure, she had slept with this old grease-ball for the past ten years because she was a money-grubbing little whore, and sure she had set up a couple of guys to rob him and get part of the take, and maybe at one time she was in love with the black guy who got away with the loot, but all that had changed since she met Mike Confidence Driscoll and now she was in love with me and wanted to have my children. Did I believe that? Not on your life, but I was still in love with her and there wasn't anything I could do about it.

"Tony," I said in my most sincere voice, "I don't know Theresa and I don't know where she is. Sorry."

"I've played poker all my life," Tony said wearily, "and I've gotten pretty good at it. You've got to read the other guy's mind, look at his face and tell what he's thinking, is he running a bluff on you or does he have the cards? I looked at your face when I told you about this ugly old wop banging her and that she had a good time and you didn't like it at all. It was a tell. You know her all right and you've banged her too. I don't hold that against you, you're a man, and any man would want to bang Theresa if he had the chance. You don't want me to get her back, and I don't blame you, but now I'm going to up the ante. I'll give you a million dollars if you'll tell me where she is and back off, just give me the chance to get her back, and if I strike out she's all yours, how about it?"

I could see why he was the capo, he was good. A million bucks. Just a couple of days ago I sent her that letter and told her I never wanted to see her again and now I'm going to turn down a million dollars and I don't even know if she likes me, let alone loves me. Sure, she fucked me, lots of times, but she does that with everyone, probably the delivery boy instead of a tip. I know what she would do if the situation was reversed, take the million and run, so why shouldn't I? You don't know if this clown is on the level, for one thing, I answered back. He connected her up with the ring and the robbery, so he figures she crossed him, and now he wants revenge. That was a possibility, I had to admit, and I hated to think of the kind of revenge Tony would dish out.

"I wish I knew her, Tony," I said. "I could sure use a million bucks, but I can't help you, you read me wrong, better brush up on your poker game."

"Maybe I better," Tony laughed. We were getting along famously. "You know, there's another way you can help even if you don't know her," Tony added. "The ring is the first hope I've had of finding her. Where was the card game where you won it?"

I told him about the only card game I could think of. "In Idaho, my old partner on the L.A.P.D. had me up and invited some retired cops over to meet me and play poker. One of them tapped out and put the ring in the pot."

Tony laughed. "Your lucky day. How much did you give him on it?"

"We figured it was a fake, the stone was too large, so we

said $1,000, take it or leave it, and he liked his hand, so he took it, but I won the pot."

Tony whistled. "Do you know how much that ring is worth?"

I lowballed, "Fifty thousand?"

"Times ten," Tony said, and then asked, "Did the man who had the ring say where he got it?"

"No."

"Was he black?"

I remembered the police report. What to say? I didn't want the mob combing Idaho and Montana looking for a black man, not so long as Mary was there, so I answered, "A black cop in Idaho? Not likely."

"How long ago was the game?"

"A week ago Saturday," I answered truthfully.

Accardo came back into the room, looked around, and asked, "Where is everybody?"

"Mike and I were having a little chat," Tony replied. "I asked the boys to step out into the hall. Why don't you call them back in?"

"Tony," Accardo said, "I asked you to let me handle this. This guy could have killed you." He left to call the others.

"Everyone thinks I'm over the hill and ready for the dump heap. I'm glad you didn't make that mistake." Tony raised his robe to show a snub-nose that he had trained on me.

"Me, too," I said and laughed. Tony joined in. We were practically buddies.

Accardo returned with the three mugs, told them to keep an eye on me, and asked Tony to come into the other room. The mugs took their same positions, two on the sofa and one behind the bar, and looked at me like they hoped I would make a move so they could pound on me again. Armani suit had gotten rid of the coat, revealing a satin sport shirt with palm trees on it and a little bit of egg on the collar.

Tony and Accardo left the room and I said to Armani suit, "There's some egg on your collar. Better wash it off before Tony sees it."

His two buddies laughed so hard I felt like Don Rickles, but Armani suit didn't think it was funny and gave me one across the mouth.

"Just trying to help," I got out through a bloody lip.

"He's right, Gino," the guy behind the bar said, "wash it off."

"It doesn't go with the palm trees," I added, and convulsed the other two again. I might be able to make it here as a comedian, I said to myself, but Armani suit still didn't think I was funny and gave me another shot to the mouth before he headed for the bathroom.

chapter thirteen

Tony and Accardo came back into the room. Tony rolled his wheelchair toward me until it bumped into my leg. He looked at me with his mean little eyes. There was no humor in them now. He opened a switchblade and pushed the point into my leg until I involuntarily pulled away.

"I'm giving you one last chance before the rough stuff, you lying son of a bitch, where is she?"

"I told you I don't know," I replied. "If I did I'd tell you, she's nothing to me, I never even met her."

Tony sighed and nodded to the three thugs. "Have it your way."

The one at the bar came over and picked me up by my two arms cuffed behind my back and held me there like a punching bag.

"Me first," Armani suit said. He moved in front of me and set up like a prize fighter, which he probably had been. He was somewhere around forty, dark with curly black hair and not bad looking except for scar tissue around his right eye and ear, which meant he was a sucker for a left hook. He had the first three buttons of the satin shirt open to show off a broad chest and a heavy gold chain with a gold medal of some saint on it. He looked like he had taken one too many punches and I hoped someone would pull him off me, because I could tell from his eyes that he enjoyed beating the crap out of someone and he wouldn't quit on his own. To make it worse, he had a grudge against me so this would be pure pleasure to him, not work at all.

I turned my head to Tony. "You know, I did meet a girl last week but her name wasn't Theresa."

"Hold up, Gino," Tony said to Armani suit, then said to me, "What did she look like?"

I described Mary except that I gave her auburn hair instead of blonde.

"She's dyed her hair," Accardo volunteered.

"Shut up, Bill," Tony said without looking at him, "I want to handle this myself. Did she have any identifying marks?"

What the hell is this all about, she was perfect, should I tell him that? Then I remembered something that made her even more perfect, just one little flaw, if you could call it that, but cute as hell.

"She had a small mole on the right cheek of her ass." Then I added to drive the point home, "I saw it when she got out of bed and walked to the bathroom and I remember kidding her about it."

"Was her pubic hair auburn too?"

Nice try, Tony, I thought, but you and I both know it was black.

"No," I answered. "When she stood in front of me naked I told her it was easy to see that she dyed her hair."

Tony looked like I had hit him and that was a tell, in his words, that it hurt to picture her with another man.

"What did she say her name was?"

I saw this coming and said, "Samantha Jones," using the name of a prostitute I once was very fond of who was probably now dead from a bad crack habit that she couldn't shake.

"Where was this?"

Oh, God, I thought, this isn't easy, I said I met her last week and I told him I was at Five's playing poker last week, what do I say now?

"She was with the guy who tossed the ring in the pot at the poker game. They had a big fight because he lost the ring. He split and she came on to me. We were together a couple of days and she tried to get me to give the ring back to her. When I wouldn't do it she got mad and took off."

"Did she say where she was going?"

I remembered the newspaper clipping and took some time to answer so it would look like I was searching for what she said.

"Florida, I think," I finally answered, "she said she was from there."

"Why didn't you tell us about this girl before?"

"You kept asking about Theresa and her name wasn't Theresa, I didn't connect it up. Also you said she was so great in bed and I didn't think she was anything special."

"That couldn't have been Theresa," Armani suit interjected, and I heard the mug behind me groan.

Tony turned to look at him. "How would you know, Gino?" he asked softly.

Gino got sweaty, just like that. The fear in him was palpable in the room.

"I heard you talk about her, boss, you always said she was the best piece of ass you ever had and that you had plenty, so I knew she must be good."

"You weren't talking from experience, were you, Gino?" Tony asked in the same soft voice.

"No, no, boss," Gino replied, "on my mother's grave I

never did it to her."

"Your mother's dead, Gino? You should have told me, I remember her from Jersey, you never told me she died, I would have gone to her funeral."

Gino looked so confused I almost felt sorry for him. "She's not dead, boss," Gino said, "I would have told you and we'd be honored to have you at her funeral, but she hasn't died yet although she hasn't been feeling too good lately, I just meant that if she was dead I would swear on her grave."

"You better not be lying," Tony said in the same soft voice, then his voice rose, "because if you are I'll personally cut off your cock and stuff it down your throat. *Capisce*?"

"Sure, boss, sure," Gino answered, the relief showing on his face now that it looked like he was going to keep his cock where it belonged for a while. "I'd never lie to you."

Tony turned his chair to face Accardo. "Let's go into the other room, Bill." He nodded at me. "You guys keep an eye on him while we're gone."

What in hell are they talking about in there, I wondered, it was like going into a huddle to call the next play.

They came back into the room and the mugs sprang back into position, with me being held up like a punching bag again.

"I think you know where she is, Mike," Tony said real friendly-like, "and I'm going to ask you to tell us."

"Someplace in Florida is all I know, Tony."

Tony nodded at Armani suit and he buried his fist in my stomach, forgetting all about what had happened before. The stomach responded with whatever was left after losing the egg and it made an ugly mess on the satin shirt with the palm trees. Armani suit went crazy, I had been nothing but trouble for him, and he went for my head screaming curses at me. I heard Accardo yelling and Armani suit was pulled off me still cursing.

"This man is in my custody, I can't allow you to abuse him," Accardo yelled at the top of his voice, "and I'm taking him out of here with me."

Better late than never.

"What the hell is this all about, Bill?" Tony asked. "We're just trying to get the truth out of him."

"Not while he's my prisoner, Tony," Accardo replied. "I'm responsible for his safety and I'm taking him to the station. Now tell your boys to back off."

Hey, maybe I was wrong about this guy, I thought, as Tony gave the order to let us go.

"Don't forget to get my ring back, Bill," I said through swollen lips.

"It's not yours, it belongs to the insurance company," Accardo replied.

"Well, get it back from him then," I said, looking at Tony.

"Like hell," Tony said, looking at the ring on his pinky finger, "this is my good luck ring, everybody knows me by it, I've had it forever and I'm not giving it back to nobody."

Accardo gave me a dirty look and said, "It's a civil matter, I'll let Tony and the insurance company sort it out, but the ring sure as hell doesn't belong to you, Mike."

We walked out of the penthouse suite of the Capri and when we were outside Accardo turned to me, furious.

"Do you have a fucking death wish?" he asked. "What was that crap about the ring? Big Tony's not a guy to fuck with, even in a wheelchair."

"All I know is that I had the ring this morning and now I don't have it. I just got taken for a ring worth a half a million bucks, that's the way I see it, and now Tony's got the ring and he's got the insurance money too."

"And you're still alive, don't forget that."

He had a point, but I noticed he didn't challenge Tony keeping both the ring and the insurance money and I knew he would never report the ring to the insurance company. The civil matter was over and Tony had won.

"Your nose is bleeding," Accardo said, handing me a handkerchief. "We'd better go out the back way. You're a mess."

That was true. My stomach hurt, my left eye was closed, my right eye was closing, and my face was swollen. I held the hankie up to my nose but the blood wouldn't stop. We took the back elevator down to the casino level and Accardo led me out of the hotel through the locker rooms used by employees to change for their shifts. I heard a voice and Sally was in front of us.

"Mike, what happened to you? Are you all right?" she asked.

"I've been better," I admitted as Accardo took my arm and kept me walking toward the exit.

"He fell down the stairs," Accardo said matter-of-factly. "I'm taking him to emergency."

"That's awful," Sally said. "Is there anything I can do to help?"

"No, but thanks for asking," I said and tried to smile but it hurt and I winced instead.

"I'm sorry you fell," she called after us. "I hope you're okay."

"Thanks. I'm gonna be fine," I said over my shoulder.

I walked on with Accardo and she held one hand up to her mouth and waved with the other one. She looked like she was going to cry again.

"You're quite the ladies' man," Accardo commented as we walked out of the hotel.

I didn't reply and we walked in silence to his car. Once inside I thanked him for getting me away from Tony and his thugs before they killed me.

"Do you need to go to the hospital?" he asked.

"Naw," I replied, "cops in L.A. all look like this. It goes

with the territory."

He laughed briefly, then said, "Look, when we get to the station I'm going to do a little paper work and release you. I thought at first I could make you as one of the scum-bags that robbed Tony, maybe the shooter, because you had Tony's ring and that was taken in the robbery, but I called L.A. and you were still on the force and working on the day of the robbery and that sounds like a pretty good alibi to me."

"I'm glad I didn't call in sick that day. There was a lot of the blue flu going around."

Accardo looked annoyed. "I'm not a funny man like you, maybe that's why I made detective and you didn't, but that's water under the bridge."

I thought better of reminding him that there wasn't much water in Las Vegas and he continued on.

"Here's some advice from one cop to another, you can take it or leave it. When I cut you loose you're on your own and I don't think Big Tony is finished with you. He'll probably try to have his boys pick you up and it wouldn't be healthy for you if he got hold of you again. If I was you I would get out of town like a scalded dog and stay out of town."

I didn't say a word the rest of the way to the station. I got the message loud and clear, and when Accardo cut me loose I caught a cab to the Barbary Coast and got out at the side door to avoid the doorman. I decided not to go to the room, there was nothing in it I needed anyway, and I headed straight for the garage. The car was where I left it on Friday, the door opened and closed with that nice solid Mercedes sound and I breathed a sigh of relief.

I wheeled up to the parking kiosk and pulled some bills from the roll the cashier had given me. The attendant looked at me and asked, "Are you sure you can drive?"

I had forgotten how I must look with one eye shut and the other almost shut and my face covered with blood. I should have gone to the room to clean up but it was too late now.

"It's not as bad as it looks," I answered. "I fell down some stairs."

The kid grinned and handed me my change, the gate went up and I drove out onto the strip, seeing out of only one eye, leaving Las Vegas, on the road, heading back to where Mary was, only I told her that I wasn't going to see her again and would leave her car with Sam, but this was Monday and my buggy wouldn't be ready until late Tuesday at the earliest, so I would have to stay overnight with her. It was fate, destiny, we were meant to be together, you name it, I felt wonderful, my aches and pains were gone.

Fate my ass, a voice answered back, you just woke up from a binge this morning, Mr. Recovering Alcoholic, and now you're going back on your word again, you make me sick. But I still love her, I replied, I knew it when I couldn't kiss Sally. I didn't know I loved her when I said that I would never see her again, I was mad at her, you can't hold me to something I wrote in anger. The hell I can't, the voice said, the reasons why you were mad at her are still there, they didn't go away, and they're good reasons, she's a lying, two-timing little tramp and she'll break your heart. Look at Tony, he just found out she slept with Gino, who's in love with his Armani suit, she'll sleep with anyone, you said so yourself. Okay, okay, I said, you win, I'll drive until it gets dark then stop some place to clean up and get some sleep, I feel terrible, maybe a good night's sleep will help.

I pulled into a motel on the outskirts of Salt Lake City. It wasn't much but it was getting dark and it was hard to see out of my right eye, which was almost closed by now. There was a coffee shop next door but all I wanted to do was fall in bed and sleep and that's what I did. There would be plenty of time for breakfast in the morning.

THE CAPO'S MISTRESS

I slept like a rock all night and woke around eight in the morning when the maid knocked on my door to see if I had hit the road and the room was empty. I yelled that I was still here and started to get out of bed but dropped back on the mattress. Everything hurt. I looked at my pillow and saw that I had bled during the night and tried again to get out of bed, this time rolling out of the sack instead of trying to sit up. I made it and staggered into the bathroom, feeling like the walking dead, but still not prepared for what I saw in the mirror. My face was caked with blood, both eyes were black and swollen and my nose looked like it might be broken. I had taken some beatings in my life, it went with the territory of being a cop, dish out pain and receive it, but I couldn't remember ever looking like this and it shocked me awake. I turned on the shower as hot as I could stand it and stood there with the water pouring down on me for what seemed like an hour. It helped and I toweled off and looked for my shaving stuff and remembered that I was in such a sweat to get out of Las Vegas that I didn't go back to the room. No razor, not even a toothbrush. Oh, well, my mouth and face were swollen and sore and it probably would have hurt like hell to shave and brush my teeth anyway.

I was hungry, which was a good sign, and then I remembered that I hadn't eaten since yesterday morning and that my breakfast had been used to decorate an Armani suit. I headed for the Happy Acres Coffee Shop and opened the door and it was one of those scenes where everyone stops eating at once and turns to look at what the cat dragged in. I was glad there were no small children present because I was sure they would have started crying. I picked a seat at the counter way back in the corner and looked at the menu. There was the cowboy breakfast with steak, three eggs, potatoes, beans, salsa and garlic bread, which sounded wonderful if I didn't have to chew it, but I did, so I settled on oatmeal and a soft boiled egg, hoping this one would stay put.

The waitress came over and I could tell by the way she looked at me that she was about to ask what the other guy looked like, so I beat her to the punch and told her not to ask what the other guy looked like and gave her my order. That didn't sit well with her and she let my order sit under the heat lamp while she talked with another waitress until I had to ask for it. It was going to be one of those days.

I filled up the Mercedes and left Happy Acres a little after nine-thirty and figured I would be at Sam's garage around three p.m. My car might not be ready that early, I told myself, so maybe I should stop along the way and pick up a razor and toothbrush and clean up a little. In case you run into Mary, I asked back, you surely wouldn't want her to see you looking like this, she might not fall into your arms and beg you to take her back, the poor fallen woman, and promise you she would be faithful to you forever. Okay, okay, I can do without the sarcasm, I answered, I'll drive straight through, bad breath and all, but you had me wrong, I wasn't thinking about Mary. I laughed out loud in reply, even though it hurt my mouth.

I made good time and pulled into Sam's garage at two forty-five. My car was in the lot with the front wheel on and looked fit and ready. Why did I feel disappointed, I asked myself, but didn't bother to answer. Sam was in the office reading the paper and the garage was empty. I felt the roll of bills in my pocket and wondered how much I would have left when Sam finished with me.

"Hello there, young fellow," he said, "I've been expecting you. Mary has called three times already. I promised I'd let her know the minute you got in. She wants to talk to you and thinks you're going to leave without seeing her. Did you two have a fight? Say, what happened to your face?"

My heart started to race and the pains and aches left me just like that. I felt wonderful. Oh, God, I love her, I can't leave her, I've got to be with her, I don't care what she's done or what she does to me, I can't let her go. Oh, yes you can, the voice said, we've been all through this and you agreed. Be a man for once, walk away while you still have a chance. I put my hand to my bruised face.

"Would you believe me if I told you there were three of them, Sam?"

"If you say so. Mary's going to make over you when she sees you."

"Don't call her, Sam. We didn't have a fight exactly but it's best that we don't see each other again."

"If you say so," Sam said again, "but are you sure you know what you're doing? She's a mighty fine-looking woman. I don't imagine many men would walk out on her."

"No, I guess not," I sighed. "Do you have a screwdriver? I want to change the plates back from her car to my car."

"I'll help you," Sam said, handing me a screwdriver. "You take the plates off the Mercedes."

The screwdriver weighed a ton in my hand, two tons, I could barely lift it. I went to the rear license plate and took it off, each turn of the screwdriver wrenching my heart. I got the plate off and started to lay it down when I saw the bug on the back of the plate. At first I didn't know what it was and looked at it dumbly, wondering where it had come from. Then it hit me. I had been used to lead them to Mary. That's what the meetings in the other room between Tony and Accardo were all about.

This ugly little thing was sending out a signal even as I looked at it, telling the world where I was. How far were they behind me? Around the corner watching me now? Turning off the freeway into Virginia City? Back in Las Vegas in Accardo's office laughing at the dumb street cop who was making their job easy? I had led them to Virginia City and to Mary, I was a dumb street cop and Mary was as good as dead. I had maybe minutes to save her, I didn't know how much time, I had to warn her, I had to get her out of town. The only thing I had going for me was that they didn't know I had found the bug. I put the license plate back on, being careful not to disturb the bug, and ran to my car in the lot. Sam had both Nevada plates off and was waiting for my plates.

"What's the rush, young fellow?" he asked, smiling. "Everybody's in a hurry these days. Take your time and smell the roses."

"Sam, this is important," I almost screamed at him. "Put those plates back on and tell me how much I owe you. I need to take my car out right now and I'll come back and pick up Mary's car."

"It'll only take me a minute to put the right plates on," he said, looking at me like I was crazy, and I didn't blame him a bit. "Let's get the job done and we won't have to do it again. Just calm down, son, I know you're upset about Mary and all but haste makes waste."

I wanted to kill him but I took a deep breath and said, "Sam, this is very important. Can you keep a secret?"

"Why, sure, son," he answered, "have you found another girl? I won't tell Mary or anyone."

"No, Sam, I haven't found another girl, but this is about Mary. She's in danger and I put her there and I need your help. Will you help me?"

Sam was all ears now. This was better than the vigilantes hanging the sheriff and he wanted in on it.

"Sure, I'll help you, son," he replied. "What do you want me to do?"

"Some men may come here later today or maybe tomorrow asking about me or Mary. They'll describe her to you and they may say her hair is auburn and call her Theresa. They're looking for the both of us but particularly for Mary. I want you to tell them that you never heard of her and don't know anyone that fits her description. They will know that Mary's car stopped here so tell them that you remember the car, a big red Mercedes, that the guy who was driving it looked like he had been in a fight, and that you filled the car with gas and the guy took off and you had never seen him before. Can you remember that?"

"Sure, I can remember that. The last time anyone came through here looking for someone was a mob from Shelby, Montana, looking for Jack Dempsey and Doc Kearns. They had a championship fight up in Shelby and old Jack and Doc took off with the receipts. The townsfolk got pretty mad and came looking for them but they never did catch them. Some folks say..."

"Some other time, Sam," I interrupted, "the men may be right behind me and I've got to move fast. Fill up the Mercedes while I put these plates back on and I'll be back to pay you what I owe you," I paused, "and thanks for your help."

"Nothing to thank me for, son, happy to do it. Maybe these fellows that are coming will have time to take a look at Old Town and hear about the Civil War and that the original settlers here were from the South. Did I ever tell you that?"

"Sure did, Sam, it was very interesting."

I put the Nevada plates back on my clunker and jumped in. What a shock after driving the Mercedes. It was a 1989 Chevy and the odometer had stopped running at 157,523 miles. Rust had done its dirty work around the bottom of the doors and was showing through the paint, what there was of it. I had packed for the trip by putting what I couldn't get in my duffel bag in open cardboard boxes on the back seat. Mary would probably change her mind the minute she saw it. The car was an eloquent statement of what life would be like with a retired cop, or even a deputy sheriff.

Sam had filled the tank and it was ready to roll. I eased out of the driveway and headed for Mary's house, hoping she was home. I caught my breath when I saw the little house again, perfect except for the lack of a white picket fence, and I pulled up in front and ran to the door. I pounded on the door and waited, then pounded again.

Mary opened the door and screamed. My God, did I look that bad? I stepped inside and grabbed her.

"Mary, Mary, it's me, Mike."

She came back to her senses. "Mike, it's you. They hurt you. Oh, Mike, forgive me, I'm so sorry. I love you so much."

She covered me with kisses and her soft lips hurt when she touched the bruises on my face but I didn't mind the pain. It was wonderful to hold her and feel her kisses, I had missed her so much, but then I thought of why I was there and pushed her away to tell her that we had to get out of Virginia City.

She misunderstood. "Mike, I know you're angry and I don't blame you, but please don't go. I love you, Mike, don't go. Sit down and listen to me. Please."

"Mary, we don't have time. I was tricked in Las Vegas and I think I'm being followed. I'm sorry, but I was stupid, I am stupid, and now Tony will know where you are unless we move fast."

She heard the urgency in my voice. "What is it, Mike? What happened?"

"They bugged your car and I didn't find out about it until I was changing the plates at Sam's garage a few minutes ago. I've got to make them think I just stopped here for gas but

I've already been here too long and I can't take a chance that they won't find out you're here. I'm going back and drive your car off into Montana someplace and I want you to take my car and get out of Virginia City by the back roads. Don't use the highway. You might be spotted."

"Where will I go?"

"I'd send you to my ex-partner's place but they already know about him and that's the first place they'd look. Just go someplace and lay low. You have to leave right now. I'm probably being followed and I don't know how far they are behind me. They might be coming up the street now. You have to be gone in five minutes."

"I'm not going anyplace without you."

"We can't go together. I'm the decoy."

"Then tell me where to go and promise you'll meet me there; otherwise, I'm not leaving. If I can't be with you I don't care if they find me."

"Mary, be reasonable."

"No. I mean it, Mike. You found out I'm a liar but I'm telling you the truth now. I didn't know I was in love with you when you left or I would never have let you go, but I do now. I'm not going unless I know you'll be there. Now tell me where we'll meet."

"I don't know where I'm going, Mary, I'm trying to lead them away from you, that's all, I can't think that fast." I smiled. "I told you I was stupid."

"Where, Mike, where do you want me to go?"

I thought, and said, "The Old Faithful Lodge in Yellowstone. The police running team stopped there once. It's an old railroad hotel right at the geyser, it's beautiful. People honeymoon there."

"Then that's what we'll do, Mike. You asked me to marry you, remember, we'll get married at Old Faithful. What a great name for a place to get married, I'll be faithful to you forever."

I melted like a popsicle in the sun. We would be faithful to each other forever and we sealed it with a kiss. The kiss hurt because my lips were cut and swollen but it was the best kiss I ever had.

"You'll get there first because I don't know where I'm going or how long I'll be. Use cash and check in as Mary Cooney, that was my mother's maiden name, can you remember that? I'll call you under that name."

"Uh-huh, will she like me?"

"She's dead but she would have loved you. She liked excitement. Here are the keys to the car, I'll run back to Sam's. Give me a quick kiss for the road and be out of here in five minutes."

"But I've got to pack my trousseau."

"You look beautiful just as you are," I said.

She looked in the mirror over the fireplace and tried to fix her hair, then she gave up and started to pull things out of the closet and throw them on the bed.

I ran down the hill to Sam's garage and asked if Mary's car was ready to go.

"Sure is, young fella, full tank of gas and I checked the oil."

I paid my bill out of the cash in my pocket. It wasn't as bad as I had expected from a garage with only one customer and I thanked Sam, then reminded him that he had never seen me before, if anyone asked, and that he had never heard of Mary or a girl named Theresa who looked like her. He waved good-bye as I rolled down the driveway and out into the street without a clue where I was going.

chapter fourteen

I drove down the highway trying to figure out what to do. It was almost four o'clock and in a couple of hours it would be dark. Probably pulling into a motel for the night would be a good idea. It was what I did last night, and it would seem natural and buy more time for Mary. I watched the Montana sky dappled with clouds disappear and saw the moon start to rise surrounded by millions of stars and in the distance the lights of Bozeman. I was in the country, nothing around me, one car on the highway in the dark, with Bozeman like an ocean liner full of lights in front of me.

I sure wasn't in L.A. In L.A. the lights never stopped. You went from one little city to another but you couldn't tell when you were leaving one and entering the next. The boundaries were political, not geographical. In Montana you left a city or town and were plunged into the darkness and you could drive for miles with the stars and moon overhead before the lights of a town appeared as a glow on the horizon.

I picked out the first motel I came to in Bozeman and

drove in. There were only a few cars and most of the rooms were dark.

"Hi," I said to the man who came to the desk when I hit the bell. He started pulling out the registry card for me to sign. "I need a room for the night overlooking the highway."

He looked up at me to see if I was kidding. "Most people want the rooms in back, there's a nice view and they're quieter. Same price."

"I can't sleep if it's too quiet. That's why I need the highway."

"Suit yourself," he said. I paid for the room and he handed me the key.

When I got inside I opened the blinds, pulled a chair up to the window, and turned out all the lights. I didn't know whether I was being followed or simply tracked electronically from Las Vegas, and it was time to find out. There was a diner across the way serving barbeque and I could smell the wood smoke and the food cooking and watch the happy customers going in and out. It was a hard wait and I was just about to give up and get some ribs when I saw a black limo go by, turn around and drive slowly past the motel, then come back and drive into the parking lot and past the Mercedes. There they are, I said to myself, and looked at my watch. I had been in the room a little over an hour. I watched the limo drive away then headed across the street for some country cooking. When I got back I asked the clerk what the next big town was and he said Billings.

"Does it have an airport?"

"Of course," he said in a hurt tone of voice, as if to tell me that this wasn't the sticks, no matter what I thought.

I made reservations to Minneapolis/St. Paul from Billings, and return, for Mr. and Mrs. Mike Driscoll, Flight 32, leaving at ten the next morning, and figured my time so I would arrive at the airport fifteen minutes before the flight, which was cutting it pretty close but I didn't have any luggage to check. It went like clockwork. Wednesday morning I made a stop in a residential area and waited about five minutes to make it look like I was picking somebody up, then I high-tailed it to the airport in Billings and left the Mercedes in the parking lot.

When the girl at the ticket counter asked where my wife was and said that she couldn't release her ticket without identification, I told her that she had morning sickness and was in the ladies' room and would meet me at the departure gate, and could she please show her identification there because we were on our way to her folks' house and they didn't know she was pregnant and we couldn't miss the flight because they would be waiting for us at the airport and we wanted to surprise them. I said it all in a hurry and kind of flustered and she asked if it was our first baby and I said it was and we were so happy because we were older and were surprised when she got pregnant. She handed me the two tickets and wished us well and I thanked her for being so understanding and ran to the gate. I boarded the plane on my ticket and left the other ticket in my pocket. My wife, whoever she was, wouldn't show up in the on board count but no one looks at those things unless the plane crashes. I looked out the window as the plane cleared the runway and thought I saw the black limo turning into the parking lot.

The bad part of my plan was that I would be trapped in the airplane for a couple of hours. I figured that the goons would find out what flight I was on and that I had bought two round trip tickets to Minneapolis/St. Paul, which would mean two things, neither of which was true: that Mary was with me on the airplane and that we were coming back to Billings. It gave Tony and Accardo, if they bought into it, the option of simply waiting for us in Billings on Sunday, the day of our return flight. That would be tempting because it was so easy but Accardo could have us picked up in Minneapolis/St. Paul on a hold from Las Vegas and he had time to make the call. I had to assume that was what he would do and that the police would be looking for a guy with a beat-up face and a good-looking blond or redhead on his arm. I looked around the airplane for good-looking women with guys and spotted two couples who qualified. Neither of the guys had his lights punched out recently but they would have to do. I got up to go to the john and on the way back I looked both women over carefully. One gave me a nice smile in return, the other did not. The flirt would be Mary, I thought ruefully, and went with her.

They were seated in back of me and when the plane landed I picked up a newspaper from the seat next to me and pretended to read it until they were beside me, then got up and stood behind them waiting to get off. She noticed, he didn't, and she kind of looked over her shoulder at me as she turned to leave the plane, as if to say thanks for the attention, I don't get enough from the guy I'm with in case you're interested.

Sure enough, the police were there and they spotted the blonde immediately and took the couple to one side to ask for identification. I was right behind them with my bruised face buried in the newspaper, pretending to read it like I had bet the farm on the daily double and was looking for the winners, walking past them waiting for the call to stop, but it never came. They were looking for a couple and I was all alone. I breezed out of the terminal and caught the first cab in line.

"Where to?" the cabbie asked.

"Drop me off downtown, I'll take it from there."

"Never been here before, have you?"

"No. How did you know?"

"Which downtown do you want?"

I couldn't tell him it didn't make any difference to me so I said Minneapolis. When he dropped me off I got a phone book and called a travel agent.

"I've got a few days to kill and I've never seen Yellowstone. Do you have anything that would get me there and back by next Sunday evening? I've got a meeting here in town first thing Monday."

He told me that he didn't have any tours that short and I asked him to suggest something.

"Why don't you fly down and back, I can book you in and out of Jackson Hole and you can rent a car."

I wanted to stay away from the airport so I said, "I'm ashamed to admit it but I'm afraid of flying. Me and John Madden."

"Lots of people are, nothing to be ashamed of. You could go by train or bus."

"Whatever drops me off closest to Old Faithful. That's what I want to see."

"Let me take a look."

He was gone for a few minutes then came back on the line. "The Trailways schedule is best for you. I can get you out tomorrow morning to West Yellowstone and back in town Sunday at six."

I picked up the ticket, got a hotel room close to the terminal and called Mary to tell her I would be on my way to Yellowstone tomorrow. Her room didn't answer so I left a message.

chapter fifteen

I got into West Yellowstone late Thursday and caught a cab to the Old Faithful Lodge. It was as I remembered it, a fairy tale lodge made of wood, but such wood, shaped and polished and reflecting the candles and lights of a lobby that soared toward the heavens. The Capri and the Venetian and the others were beautiful and luxurious in their own way, but that was new money and the nouveau riche. This was old money, the Morgans and the Astors and the Carnegies, gone now and belonging to another time, an old hotel full of ghosts and dance cards and the many hearts that were broken after the ball was over.

I called Mary from the lobby and she gave me the room number and was waiting at the elevator door when it opened. I was hugged and kissed before the elevator doors closed and cut off the view of the nice old couple sharing the ride up with me. "Oh. Mike, Mike, I've missed you so much. I've been afraid to go outside the room. I didn't know what to do."

"What's the matter?"

THE CAPO'S MISTRESS

She showed me a newspaper article about the murder of somebody named Herbert Adams and next to the article was a picture of the little house, a picture of Adams and a picture of Mary. He had been killed when he came to pick her up to go on a hayride yesterday. So he was dead, so what? I wanted to know why she had a date to go on a hayride with him and I wanted to know now.

"Is this some guy you were seeing behind my back?" I yelled at her, all the doubts flooding back.

"Don't yell at me. He came to collect the rent last Saturday after I got your letter saying you never wanted to see me again, and he found me crying. I told him about the letter and said I wanted to die. He was very nice and invited me to go on the hayride to cheer me up. I forgot all about it when you showed up at the door. All I had to do was call him and tell him I couldn't make it. I killed him. He was such a nice old man, like a father to me. Look at his picture."

She started to cry. I looked at the picture again and felt awful. He was old and he was ugly and I had the nerve to think Mary was playing around with him. How stupid can a guy get? I tried to put my arm around her shoulder and she pushed it away.

"Go away. You're hateful."

"Mary, I'm sorry. It's just that the thought of you with another man drives me crazy. Please forgive me."

"No. You don't trust me. How could you think I'd cheat on you?"

"I'm jealous, that's all, jealous because I love you. Give me a little kiss." She did, just a peck.

"They were after me, not Mr. Adams, that's the reason I showed you the article. I can't let them find me and now my picture is on the front page of every newspaper. I didn't go outside the room today because I was afraid someone would recognize me and call the police. I can't let them arrest me.

Tony will find out where I am and he can get to me. He's done it before."

"Who's seen you?"

"The doorman, and the desk clerk when I checked in, and I had dinner in the dining room Tuesday night. I walked around the hotel a little bit but I didn't have dinner last night. I wasn't feeling well, I think I'm catching a cold. This morning I had room service. That's when I saw the paper."

"Did you see Old Faithful?"

"No. I walked out Tuesday night after dinner but it was too cold to wait around for it to go off."

"We've got to get out of here. Too many people have seen you. We'll check out first thing in the morning and stop by the geyser on our way."

We had dinner in the room and went right to bed but we didn't make love. Instead, in the dark, like in a confessional, I said, "Mary, I'd like you to tell me what really happened. No more lies, that's important. I don't care what you did, we're going to start fresh, but I want the truth. If I find out you've lied to me I'm walking. I've got to be able to trust you no matter how much I love you. How did the sack of money get into the lagoon?"

"Mike, I'm not ready for this," she protested. "I'm going to tell you but I need more time to think out what really happened. I've told so many lies I'm not sure of the truth anymore."

She's good, I told myself, she's trying to give herself a little wiggle-room. Well, to hell with that, I went to Las Vegas and I got the goddamn bag for her and I want to know what it's all about. Right now. She doesn't have any idea how much I know or that I've read the crime file. All she knows is that I found out her story was phony. The best way to find out if she's still trying to con me is for me to ask the questions and for her to give the answers.

"I know quite a bit about what happened, Mary, so rather than make you try to remember the whole thing again, why don't I fill myself in by asking you questions about it?"

"Fine, Mike, let's do it that way."

"Okay. Who was the black man and where is he now?"

"There was no black man," she laughed. "I read that in the papers after I got to Virginia City. Tony made it up."

"Why would he do that?"

"Because he wanted to make it look like a robbery too. If it was a robbery there was insurance, but most of all he couldn't tell the police he shot Marc Gambino when he found him in bed with me. Not only would he be arrested and face a trial that would be a media circus, but if by some miracle he got off he would have to face the Gambino family in New Jersey. They're very powerful in the organization. It might be okay to kill Marc if Tony found him in bed with his wife, then Tony's honor would be involved, but a mistress? No way. The family would be entitled to avenge his death and they would and nobody would stop them."

I was confused. "Then there was no robbery?"

"No."

"But who took your jewelry and the money and the ledger?"

"Me."

"Why?"

"Because I shot Tony and thought I had killed him. I was in the same position he was. His wife and children hate me for taking him away from them. That's why he came to Las Vegas, to get away from them. He sees them once or twice a year but that's it. If I killed him I was as good as dead so I had to make it look like he got shot in a robbery."

"How did you do it?"

"He had been to a meeting of the families in New Jersey and was supposed to be gone ten days. He came back three days early and that's how we got caught. The first thing he does when he's been away is pick up the skim money from Secci, the head cashier, and bring it upstairs to put in the room safe for distribution. That's why he was carrying a gun, he had about two hundred fifty thousand in the bag, and that made me think of a robbery."

"Wait a minute, you're going too fast for me. What's the skim money and who was going to get it?"

"Gambling is a cash business. Tony takes about ten million a year off the top that isn't reported for taxes or to anybody else. It goes to his investors. That was the deal he made with them when he built the Capri. The real estate market was down and he couldn't raise money, even from the union funds, so he went to the families. They get back what's on the books, plus interest, and they also get money under the table. I don't know when it stops. That's what the ledger is for. The money is cut up and each investor's share is recorded in the ledger, then it's laundered to offshore accounts."

"So that's what all those figures are about?"

"Yes."

"And Tony made all those entries and initialed them?"

"No. The entries and initials are mine and Tony let me skim a little off the top for doing it. That's where a lot of my jewelry came from."

"Okay, so what happened when Tony came in the room?"

"It was morning. Marc had been with me all night and we were right in the middle of, you know, when Tony walked in. He started cursing in Italian and waving his gun at us. I didn't know what he was saying but Marc did and he jumped out of bed completely naked and tried to pull his pants on. Tony kept cursing at him and then he shot him in the chest and Marc fell back on the bed. I rolled out of bed on the opposite side and tried to find the gun that Tony always keeps in the nightstand. I got it in my hand just as he turned toward me and I shot first and he fell down at the end of the bed."

"It was self defense."

"You weren't listening. The family doesn't care about self defense. I wouldn't have been alive for the trial."

"Sorry. Did you know Tony wasn't dead?"

"No. I thought I had killed him. He just fell where he was and didn't move."

"Okay, so now you think you've got two dead bodies on your hands. How do you make it look like a robbery?"

"This is the really gruesome part. I still have bad dreams about it. Marc was completely nude and I had to dress him." Her voice rose and she started to cry and rock back and forth. "We had just been making love and he was so young and alive, and now he had a hole in his chest and his eyes were staring up at the ceiling and I had to touch him and wrestle with him to get his clothes back on him. It was horrible. I don't think I can go on."

I reached over and touched her shoulder to try to comfort her but she kept rocking back and forth and crying, saying nothing. It was silent except for her sobs.

She finally looked at me in the dim light. "I have to tell you this part but it's very hard; please bear with me."

I nodded, not wanting to speak.

"When I finally had him dressed I realized his sport shirt didn't have a hole in it and the blood was staining it from underneath, so I took Tony's gun and lined it up as well as I could with the bullet hole under his shirt and shot him again, then I wiped the gun clean and put it back in Tony's hand."

Jesus, I said to myself, what if he wasn't dead either?

"What did you do then?" I asked.

"I took my gun and wiped it clean and put it in Marc's hand and pressed his fingers around it, none of Tony's guns have serial numbers, they're always filed off. Then I opened the safe and dumped everything in the canvas bag, my jewelry, the ledger book and whatever cash was in the safe, and I wiped the dial clean like a burglar would do. The maid comes in every day around eleven to make up the room and I knew she would find the bodies. I got dressed and wore a long coat to hide the canvas bag and took the back elevator downstairs so no one would see me. I didn't know what to do with the bag because I couldn't be seen with it and I was going to go shopping all day and come back in the late afternoon and then I saw the lagoon at the Treasure Island. It was the only place I could think of to get rid of the bag but I knew the water would ruin the entries in the ledger and I thought maybe I could sell it to the families whose names were in it so I went back upstairs to the room and wrapped it in plastic and put it back in the canvas bag. It was still early and I dumped the bag into the lagoon, then I needed to remember the spot where I threw it so I counted the posts. I had lunch at the Bellagio and visited all the shops and bought a lot of things so they'd remember me, then I went back to the Capri. I almost died when they told me Tony was alive but in a coma and had been taken to the hospital."

"So what did you do?"

"I went to the hospital and asked the doctors how he was doing and they told me they didn't think he'd ever come out of the coma and would probably die that night, but he didn't. I came back every day and stayed for hours waiting for him to die, then I heard the family was coming to be with him. I knew that would be the end of my visits so I pulled the plug on the respirator but all kinds of alarms went off. I told them I tripped over the cord but they never let me be with him alone again.

"After the family arrived I called the hospital several times a day to see how he was doing and one day they told me he had come out of the coma and was awake. I thought either the police or the family were on their way to get me so I threw everything I could into a bag and ran to my car and took off.

You know the rest."

"Not quite. Who was Marc Gambino?"

"He was the only son of a branch of the Gambino crime family. He was about twenty-five and he had fallen head over heels for a chorus girl in New York. I was one myself once and there's nothing wrong with that and if she was Italian it probably would have been okay, but she was Puerto Rican and the family didn't like her, so they told him they wanted him to go to Las Vegas for a while and learn the casino business from Tony. He was no dummy and he knew what was happening but he didn't want the family to cut him out of the business either so he came. Tony thought the best way to cure him of the chorus girl was to get him laid, and he was a good-looking kid with a great build, so Tony started him as a lifeguard at the pool and told him he would move him up from there.

"The girls went absolutely crazy for him, showgirls, guests at the Capri, daughters of guests, all of them, they would hang around him at the pool and take off their tops and ask him to rub on their sunscreen, it was quite a show, but he wouldn't give them a tumble. He said he had a girl in New York and left it at that. I think he knew what Tony was trying to do.

"I couldn't help but wonder if I could get him in bed, it was like a challenge. I started going to the pool early in the morning before there was a crowd but I never so much as looked at him or untied the top of my bikini. I would sit there and put on my sunscreen by myself and leave around eleven. He knew who I was and one day he came up to me and asked if he could help me with the lotion. It was right after Tony left on his ten-day trip. I know that it sounds weird but I think that Marc had a plan to get even with Tony by taking me to bed. There was something about the way he first looked at Tony when he caught us and the way they were yelling back and forth in Italian. If that's right we were both after the same thing and it didn't take long. Poor Marc, he was so young."

"Is that it?"

"No. We've got the ledger and it could put the head of every crime family in jail for income tax evasion and God knows what else. It could cost Tony his life if they find out. That's why he's trying to find us, to get it back. It's got to be worth a fortune and all we have to do is name our price."

"And that's why you went back to the room to wrap it in a laundry bag?" I asked, picturing her wrapping it in the company of a guy she believed she had just shot to death and a guy she had just finished fucking, then shooting after he was already dead to put a hole in his shirt. What a money-grubbing little whore she was.

She hung her head, "Yes, I thought Tony was dead and I needed money, lots of it, for my future." She smiled at me, rolled over and kissed me, and said, "It's our future now, Mike." Then she put one of her legs across my body and rubbed herself against me, pulling me close.

I got a bad feeling. It was the same feeling I used to get when I had to write a phony report to cover for something stupid Five had done. I hated the erection she had given me and managed to say, with great effort, because I wanted her badly now, "That's called blackmail and extortion, both felonies, and I don't want to go there."

She flared and pulled the leg back. "I know what it's called and I don't give a shit. I want the money."

I winced. There was something about a woman using the word "shit," particularly the woman I loved, that demeaned her. I saw it on the force when female cops were hired for the first time. They would come on the job and start swearing a blue streak to be one of the boys and it never worked, at least with me. I always thought less of them. The erection withered away.

"We can get money, Mary, and do the right thing too by putting the bad guys away. The Treasury Department pays a percentage of what they collect on that kind of information, sometimes 10%. If they've skimmed fifty million dollars, 10% is a lot of money."

"Do they pay it up front or only after they collect?"

She knew the answer to her question when she asked it and she smiled at me in a superior sort of way that was maddening. Why was I a dunce for wanting to do it the right way? These days it's the wise guy who scores every buck he can, right or wrong, that's the hero. Whatever happened to John Wayne?

"How do you think Tony's going to react when you ask him to cough up millions of dollars?"

"No different than now. He's already trying to find me to get the ledger back. I want to make it easy for him by selling it back to him."

"Mary, I hate to say this, but I don't think that's all he wants. I think he wants to kill you too because the account book is only part of it. You made him a cripple. He wants revenge. I know I would."

We were both silent, lost in our thoughts.

Finally she spoke. "Mike, I've thought about what you said and there's only one way out. We can't stay on the run in the States like this because sooner or later Tony will hunt us down. We've got to get as much money as we can from Tony and disappear, go to South America or someplace and never come back. We can travel, go to Spain and France and all the places you've never seen. It'll be wonderful."

It didn't sound very wonderful but she had me, she was right, if we stay in the States sooner or later Tony will catch up with us. He'll probably catch up with us anyway, the world isn't that big any more, but maybe not. There goes the little house with the white picket fence. I swallowed hard because I didn't want to say it, I was back with Five again.

"How much shall we ask for?"

She kissed me and put the leg back over me. When she answered it was like we were already married. Nobody asked me if I wanted the job, but I was the negotiator.

"Start out with ten million and don't go below five."

She gave me Tony's private number and sat next to me on the bed while I called. Tony's voice answered.

"Tony, it's Mike Driscoll calling from Minneapolis. We're leaving here tonight so don't bother tracing the call."

"That's a tell, Mike," Tony laughed. "I don't know where in hell you are but I know you're not in Minneapolis. What do you want?"

"I've got something to sell, Tony, you know what it is, and it's safely put away with instructions to turn it over to the Feds if anything happens to us."

"Theresa's got to be part of the package, she knows too much."

"That's not for sale, Tony. When you buy the account book you'll never hear from us again."

"How do I know you don't have copies?"

"You don't, you'll just have to trust us."

"I wouldn't trust Theresa as far as I could throw her and you shouldn't either."

"That's my problem, Tony, let me worry about it. Are you interested in the merchandise?"

"How much?"

"Ten million."

"Call me back when you're serious," Tony said and hung up the phone. I called him a few minutes later just as he knew I would.

"I'm serious," I said. "Theresa says you've skimmed over fifty million and handed it out to all the families. This could bring down the whole organization."

"Mike, I'm your only buyer. Who else are you going to sell to?"

"The Treasury Department, we'll get a finder's fee of at least ten percent. I'm giving you first chance at it before we go to the Feds."

"Thanks, Mike, but you and I both know that the Feds don't pay off until they collect and that will be a cold day in hell. I'll give you five million if the package includes Theresa; otherwise the book is only worth a million to me. There's too big a chance she'll double cross me."

"I told you that's not negotiable. We're getting married."

"Where can I send the wedding present?"

"Save your money, you're not invited. I'll come down to eight if we can get the money right away."

"I run a cash business here, Mike, that's not a problem. I'll pay two."

"Six, and that's final."

"Four, and that's final, want to flip a coin, the loser agrees to the other's figure?"

"For two million dollars over the phone? Do you think I'm crazy?"

"Mike, I got you figured as a guy who wouldn't lie about which way the coin came up. You flip and I'll make the call from here."

"Let's split the difference at five."

"Five it is. I was right about you, Mike, if you ever need a job I've got a place for you here. Where do I pick up the merchandise?"

"Virginia City, that's where it is but don't bother to look because you'll never find it. I'm not going to move it and tip off where it's at. You'll have it when I count your money. Only one of your boys is to bring the money and I'll be alone."

"No, we each have to have a backup, one man only, that way you can count while your man keeps his eyes open, and my guy can make sure you're handing back the original ledger while his backup keeps an eye on you and your boy."

"Okay, but I'm not bringing Theresa. If anything goes wrong she's going straight to the cops with the whole story."

"I won't be there either. Where in Virginia City and when?"

"Can you have the money by noon Sunday?"

"I told you that wasn't a problem."

"We'll meet in Old Town in front of the Opera House. The whole thing is pretty much shut down this time of the year. We'll be the only ones there."

"I'll send Gino and Frankie," he laughed. "You know what they look like."

"Yes, we've met."

Tony hung up the phone.

"We've got the five million," I said to Mary.

She let out a squeal of delight and covered me with kisses. We rolled on top of each other in the middle of the bed, but then she wanted to know what Tony had said so I told her and hoped that we could get back to business but she wasn't finished with me.

"You should have flipped a coin like Tony wanted to. We'd have six million instead of five."

"What if I lost the flip?"

"You couldn't lose, dummy, Tony couldn't see your coin."

"But he trusted me."

She kissed me gently, as you would a lovable but slow child.

"Mike, Mike, you've got a lot to learn. I'm coming with you to Virginia City."

"No, you're not. It's too dangerous."

"Yes, I am. I told you the ledger was in Virginia City but I didn't tell you where."

"Mary, be reasonable."

"I am being reasonable. Five million dollars is a lot of money. I want to be there when you get it."

"You don't trust me?" I asked incredulously.

"I trust you, darling, but I don't trust the people you're meeting. I'll be your backup."

"No way, I hate to say this but that's just plain dumb. As soon as you, me and the books are in one place they'll blast us. They won't go after me and the ledger in one place if you're in another because they know you'll turn them in and they don't know where you are. That's the only way the exchange will work."

"Who's going to be your backup then?"

"I'll have to ask my ex-partner. He's a hell of a shot and he's the only one I can think of that I can trust. I'll have to pay him."

"How much?"

"I thought I'd offer him one hundred thousand dollars."

"What?" Mary screamed. "For five minutes work? Are you out of your mind?"

"Mary, he could get killed, you of all people know who we're dealing with."

"Tony's never paid that kind of money on a contract in his whole life, and that's for killing somebody."

"How much then?"

"Fifty thousand tops."

"I'll call him and see if he's interested. If he is and he thinks it's safe I'll ask him if we can stay at his place tomorrow night. When we get the money on Sunday we'll get the hell out of here."

"It can't come soon enough for me. After Sunday I never want to see Virginia City again."

She went into the bathroom and I called Five. I asked if anyone had called or been around asking for me and he said no but that someone had broken into his house while he was away and killed his dog. All he talked about when I visited him was Blackie, how smart she was and how Blackie loved to go hunting with him, and I told him that I was sorry and that I probably knew who killed Blackie and what they were after.

"Tell me who they are. No one will blame me for what I do to them when I find them."

"Did you read in today's paper about the man who was murdered in Virginia City? The ones who killed him are the ones who shot Blackie. I told them I was with you last week."

"What's it all about?"

I thought for a minute. What was it all about? "It's about a woman, Tom, a woman I've fallen in love with. She used to be with Tony Danzante and she has an account book that he wants. He's willing to pay to get it back and I'm supposed to meet two of his boys on Sunday and turn the book over to them. I need you to back me up. I can pay you $50,000 out of what I collect for your trouble. Are you interested?"

"This is a book that would get him in a lot of trouble if it got in the wrong hands, am I right?"

"Yes."

"Didn't we used to call that blackmail when we were cops?"

I felt like screaming at him: It's a shakedown, you dumb fuck, that's what you did for thirty years on the force, don't lecture to me.

"Yes," I answered, "it's blackmail, is that a problem?"

"No. How much are you getting?"

I knew he'd get around to that. What shall I tell him? The truth? He'll go crazy when he hears how much it is. He was always jealous of what everyone else had.

"Five million dollars."

He whistled. "That's a lot of money, Mike."

"I know. It belongs to Mary. She's the one that has the book."

"And you're the one that has the girl, just like in the movies, and you'll live happily ever after. I saw her picture in the paper. She's quite a looker."

"Yeah, she is that. Look, if you're interested, we'd like to stay with you, then you and I can go up to Virginia City on Sunday and do the exchange. I don't want to take any more chances on hotels and motels."

"Where will she be?"

"Waiting for us at your place. They've already been there and shot Blackie so that's probably the safest place there is. She wants to come with us but I don't think it's a good idea. Are you in?"

"I don't know. I had plans for this weekend."

I knew what his plans were. I was there on a weekend: a Saturday night poker game with the boys, this time in Frank's Winnebago, where dinner will be mounds of sauerkraut and sausages with beer and pretzels and he'll get gas and fart all night. He was trying to hold me up, some things never change.

"Tom," I said, "I don't want to work a hardship on you. Are you in or out?"

"Look, Mike, I know we're friends and all, but I think $50,000 is a little light when you're picking up five million. These guys are killers. They're the ones who wasted that old guy in Virginia City, isn't that what you said?"

"Yeah, they're the ones who killed Blackie too." That was a cheap shot, why the hell did I say that?

"All the more reason I should get more money."

"What did you have in mind?"

"A hundred thousand."

That's what I wanted to give him, so why am I trying to screw someone who's supposed to be my friend out of what's fair? Mary's just going to have to live with it.

"I won't argue about it, Tom, $100,000 it is. We'll leave here tomorrow morning and cross over the Tetons to get to your place. We should be there around three or four. See you then."

chapter sixteen

In the morning we had breakfast in the room and I checked out for her and bought a paper. I opened it and there I was right on the front page along with the picture of Mary that was in yesterday's edition. My face was still bruised from the beating I had taken so I didn't think I was too recognizable, but it was a shock. The story said that we were both missing and wanted for questioning and asked anyone seeing us to notify the police but not to attempt to stop us. I slunk back to the room and showed Mary the paper, then waited with the bags while Mary checked herself in the bathroom mirror one more time. When she came out she said that she had decided to dye her hair black since the whole world, including Tony, was looking for a blonde. She would get some hair dye wherever we stopped tonight. I didn't answer and picked up the bags to leave but as I did there was a knock on the door.

We looked at each other, neither saying a word. Another knock, then a voice, "Mary, Mike, it's Bob Hill. Are you there? I've got the key and I'm coming in if you don't answer."

Mary grabbed my arm and whispered not to tell him anything, then called out, "Just a minute, Bob."

Don't tell him anything, a man was murdered in her house and she doesn't want to tell the sheriff anything, I've got to see this.

"Hello, Bob," Mary said as she opened the door, "we were just about to call you. Our pictures are in this morning's paper. Isn't it terrible about poor Mr. Adams? He seemed like such a nice old man. How did you know we were here?"

Not bad, she's put the ball into his end of the court.

"You were identified from your picture in yesterday's paper, Mary, and the hotel notified the park police. They called me because Herbert Adams was murdered in my jurisdiction and it's my case."

He looked around. "I see you're packed to leave and they told me at the desk that Mike had just settled the bill. Where were you going?"

Mary looked surprised at the question. "Why, back to Virginia City, of course, after we called you."

Too bad she didn't get in the movies, she was good.

"Can we close the door and sit down?" Bob asked.

We all drew up chairs around the table still covered with our breakfast dishes. So far I hadn't said a word and the sheriff turned to me. "What happened to your face, Mike? Looks like somebody worked you over."

I thought of my conversation with Sam Culpepper. He had to have told the sheriff.

"Three guys beat me up, Bob, but I got away from them. I led them on a wild goose chase and finally lost them by catching a plane out of Billings to Minneapolis. I was driving Mary's car and left it at the airport in Billings. It's still there."

He turned to Mary. "I never knew you had a car, Mary." It was more of a question than a statement and Mary took it that way. She smiled and managed to look embarrassed. "I was hiding it from the finance company, Bob, I was behind on my payments."

"Sam Culpepper said you called him last Monday and said that Mike was coming back from Las Vegas and for Sam to call you the minute Mike got in, is that right?"

"Yes, we had a fight and I was afraid Mike would leave my car with Sam and just take off in his car. Sam was repairing it, as you know, and it was all fixed and waiting for him." She looked at me shyly and she managed a blush. "You see, I love Mike very much and I didn't want to lose him. It was just a silly lovers' quarrel."

It was my turn. "What were you doing in Vegas, Mike?"

"I went there to get something that Mary had left behind when she came to Virginia City."

The minute I said it I knew what his next question would be. "What was that?"

To hell with it, I liked the guy and I didn't like the position Mary had put me in: Don't tell him anything, she said. That wasn't going to get us anyplace.

"It was a sack full of money."

Mary's mouth fell open and the love in her expression a moment ago vanished. I had crossed her and she didn't like it.

"That's about what Jeb said," the sheriff replied and it was my turn to look surprised. "Let me play you the tape of his interview."

He took out a cassette tape recorder, turned it on and held it up for us to hear.

"Thanks for coming in, Jeb. I guess you heard about Herb Adams."

"Yeah, but I can't say I'm too sorry. He was a carpetbagger from California trying to make a buck by building a Wal-Mart no one wanted. Now that's dead too."

"Probably, but that's no reason to feel good about him being killed. We haven't had a homicide here in forty years. I think the killers came from Las Vegas and were after Mary Carter, I don't think it was a burglary at all. You used to go with her. Can you tell me what you know about her?"

"She was from Las Vegas all right. We had quite a thing going. I fell for her real hard and I thought she felt the same way. The sex was fantastic, then she dropped me. I thought if I scared off anyone else who tried to see her she would have to come back to me, but she wouldn't have anything to do with me."

"She said that was because you hit her."

"What? That's a goddamn lie. I never hit her. That prick Mike said something like that to me too. She must have told him that, the lying bitch. No wonder he lit into me."

"What did you break up over?"

"As near as I can figure, because I couldn't swim."

"That's a funny thing to break up over. Tell me about it."

"She said she was a blackjack dealer when she was in Vegas and one night there was a holdup and one of the robbers threw a bag of money her way when he got shot and no one saw it so she threw it in some kind of lagoon and she wanted me to go to Vegas and get it. I told her I didn't know how to swim and that was the end of me. I couldn't believe it. I really liked her." He paused on the tape. "To tell you the truth, Bob, I loved her. Still do. I took it pretty hard. All I could think to do was keep any other man away from her and she would come back. I was pretty dumb, I guess. I don't know if she even liked me, she was only interested in getting that bag of money out of the water and back to her."

"Did he say he still loved me?" Mary asked innocently. She wanted to be sure I hadn't missed it.

"Yes. Did Jeb hit you, Mary?"

He had asked her that question before when he came to the house after our first night at Curly's. I wanted to hear the answer now.

"Well, what I meant was that I was afraid he was going to hit me. He has a terrible temper and I know he doubled up his fist."

"Mike, Sam said that when you came into his garage last Tuesday you told him that three men were after you and to tell them that he had never heard of Mike Driscoll or Mary or a girl named Theresa who looked like her, is that right?"

"Yes."

"How did you know that they would stop at Sam's garage?"

"I had changed the plates on Mary's car so it would look like it was from California and I was changing them back when I found a bug under the back license plate. It was then I realized I was being tailed and I told Mary to take my car and come here and I would try to lead them away from her."

"Who's Theresa?"

"Theresa Defoe. That's Mary's real name."

He turned to Mary. "Why did you use a phony name when you came here, Mary?"

"You heard what Jeb said. There was a robbery at the Treasure Island where I was a dealer and I wound up with a bag of money and threw it in the lagoon. I don't think I did anything wrong. I left the bag in the lagoon so it was still on their property. I panicked and took off when I found out that the surveillance cameras had me on tape and that made me look guilty of something. I couldn't use my real name here because I didn't know if I was wanted in Vegas."

Oh, oh, she was betting the farm that he hadn't yet found out that there was no robbery at the Treasure Island and he wouldn't find out until after Sunday when we had the five million and were long gone.

"Mary, Herbert Adams was a very prominent man and I'm getting a lot of heat from the country club people where he lived. How well did you know him?"

"Oh, hardly at all. He would come by to collect the rent, you know, and he came by right after Mike left for Las Vegas and I told him I wouldn't have the rent until Saturday because that would be when Mike came back. Then, when he came by Saturday, Mike had sent the bag of money by FedEx with a hateful note saying he never wanted to see me again, and Mr. Adams found me crying and asked if I would like to go on a hayride next Wednesday at his country club to cheer me up. It was so kind of him and I thanked him and said 'yes' and then I totally forgot about it when Mike told me I had to leave the house. I feel just terrible. If I had called him he would be alive today. The men at the house were looking for me and the sack of money."

"Where is the money, Mary?"

"I put it in a safe deposit box at the bank on Monday."

"Why were the men looking for you?"

"They knew that I had the money."

"How did they know where you lived?"

"I don't know."

The sheriff pulled a FedEx slip out of his pocket and said, "I found this in the trash. It's for a package from Las Vegas and has Mary's address on it. Did you send it, Mike?"

Oh, God, I threw all the fruit into the wastebasket and it had the name of the store on the wrappers. Accardo must have found out I bought a big box of candied fruit and figured I wanted the box, not the fruit, then checked all the package-mailing places around the hotel. He also set me up to leave town in a car he had bugged. I had to admit he was a pretty good detective. I hoped he was getting paid well by Tony.

I realized the sheriff was waiting for my answer. "Yes, I sent it. I'm just a dumb cop, I guess."

"I also found this in the trash, Mary."

He pulled a little gift card from his pocket and read the

message: "Dear Mary, Roses are red, violets are blue, sugar is sweet and I love you," then said, "It's signed 'Herbert Adams.' His secretary said he sent you roses every day starting the Thursday before his death. What was his relationship with you?"

Mary flared, "He was old enough to be my father."

I remembered my time spent testifying as a cop. That's a non-responsive answer, the judge would say. Keep going, sheriff, I want to hear this.

"Do you know Harriet Smith? She lives across the street from you."

"That old busybody. She's never away from her kitchen window looking out to see what's going on and then she gets on the telephone and passes it all over town."

"That's how I happened to find Herb Adams' body. She called me and said that three strange men had gone into your house, then Adams arrived later and the men left but he hadn't come back out. She said it looked to her like you were running a house of ill-repute and she wanted me to do something about it. I told her I was sure she was wrong but I would check the house. The door was open and when I went in everything had been pulled out and thrown on the floor like they were looking for something. I went into the bedroom and Adams was lying dead on the bed with your green robe in his arms. He had been shot twice. Harriet also said that Adams was at your house for dinner Saturday night and was carrying a bottle of champagne and he didn't leave until the next morning."

It was my turn for my mouth to fall open. The lying little bitch was bedding down someone named Herbert Adams while I was gone. The question was: Why? I had seen his picture in the paper and he *was* old enough to be her father. So was Tony but this guy was a scrawny little bastard that didn't look like he could jack himself off. It made me sick to think of him on top of her. I was glad he was dead.

Mary looked at me and she could see I was furious. She

tried a little smile as if to say, don't worry, it was nothing, I was doing geriatric research, but I turned away. If the sheriff was trying to turn us against each other, a standard cop technique, he was doing a hell of a job.

"Bob, Harriet Smith hates me. I did have Herbert Adams to dinner Saturday night to thank him for waiting for the rent money and he brought a bottle of champagne but he was out of the house by ten o'clock. He sent roses the next day to thank me for the dinner and I saw what he wrote on the card. He wasn't serious. I had a steak dinner and they serve nothing but lean cuisine at the country club. He said he loved having a real dinner for a change. That's what he meant."

It was a pretty good recovery, I give her that, but she wasn't fooling me. She had something going on with the old fart, something she was angling for, and I didn't know what it was but I would find out as soon as we were alone. I don't think Bob Hill bought it either. He changed the subject.

"Sam got a good look at the three men when they stopped at his garage, and I called a police artist from Helena to come talk to him to see if we can get some sketches of what they look like, but maybe you know who they are, Mary."

It was intended as a question, low key, like the sheriff had been watching too much Columbo, and Mary took it that way.

"I don't know, Bob. Maybe they saw Mike pull the bag out of the lagoon at the Treasure Island and recognized it as being from the robbery. It was all over the news that one bag was missing."

She was pressing her luck. It was clear that the sheriff didn't know yet that there never was a robbery at the Treasure Island, but I wouldn't have told him that it was all over the news. That was like telling him to get the tapes, then it would hit the fan.

I knew my turn was coming again and it did. "How about you, Mike? Do you know who they were?"

"They called each other Gino, Frankie and Lou but I never heard their last names."

That was a truthful answer.

"Where did they beat you up?"

"At the hotel."

Another truthful answer, only it was the Capri, not the Barbary Coast.

"What did they want?"

"They wanted the bag from the lagoon but by that time I had already sent the bag to Mary so I didn't have it."

"How did they know you had the bag at all?"

"Another dumb mistake by me. When I got the bag it was wet and I dumped it on the bed. I knew I was lucky that night and I borrowed some money to gamble and tossed everything else into the room safe when I left the room. I made quite a score and sent the bag to Mary. I had plenty of money then but I was broke by Monday. I looked in the safe to see if there was any money that had fallen out of the bag. There wasn't any money but way back in the corner there was a ring with a big diamond that I guess had fallen out of the bag. I tried to borrow money on it and I guess the cashier recognized it as part of the loot because the next thing I knew I had three goons pounding on me asking where Theresa was and where the bag was."

"What did you tell them?"

"That I didn't know any Theresa and that I had won the ring in a card game at my ex-partner's house at Henry's Lake."

"And they bought that?" Bob Hill asked incredulously.

"No. That's why they were pounding on me. I stuck to my story so I guess they bugged my car and let me go so they could follow me."

The sheriff was quiet and then said, "There's something else. They figured out that you had shipped the bag to Mary and went through the records of FedEx and probably a bunch of other shippers. That isn't easy to do without police involvement. Something's missing. Are the Las Vegas police after you, Mary?"

The sheriff was no dummy. I didn't know if the fake robbery at the Treasure Island would hold up until Sunday.

"I don't know, Bob, I left Las Vegas because I thought they would be. They had my picture on the surveillance cameras."

"But the three men that killed Herbert Adams weren't cops. At least, I hope they weren't. Why were they after you, Mary?"

"They think I double-crossed them. It was no accident that I got that bag."

Both of us looked at her, taken completely aback by that announcement. I recovered first.

"Mary, don't say anything else. You have the right to remain silent and anything you say can be used against you, do you understand me?"

She nodded and I turned to the sheriff.

"Bob, I'm sorry to say this but the interview's over. I can't let her incriminate herself. You can take us in and book us or you can let us go. I'm not aware of any criminal charges against her in Las Vegas and you know from your investigation that she had no part in the death of Herbert Adams, which is the only thing that happened within your jurisdiction."

The sheriff kind of smiled and said, "The first thing that I did after I took Jeb's statement was check Las Vegas for any warrants for her arrest and there were none. Of course, I was using the name Mary Carter, not Theresa Defoe. I'm going to have to hold her until we can run that name. I'll call the office and have them call me back here."

We waited for what seemed like forever while the wheels of justice ground exceedingly slow and exceedingly fine. Finally, the phone rang and Bob picked it up and we waited again while he listened. All he said was, "Are you sure?" He got an answer and hung up and turned to us.

"There are no warrants. You're free to go if you stay within one hundred miles of Virginia City and keep me advised of your telephone number and address at all times; otherwise, I can and will hold you as material witnesses in the death of Herbert Adams. I'll cancel the all-points."

After he left I turned to Mary, mystified. "Why did you say that? You just told the sheriff you were part of a non-existent holdup at the Treasure Island casino."

"Because he was getting too close with his questions and I had to shut him up. I took a chance that you'd do and say what you did and said, or that Bob would read me my rights. The police aren't after me in Vegas, Tony is."

chapter seventeen

I drove away from the lodge feeling as if a ten-thousand-pound weight had been lifted off me. I pulled into the turnout for Old Faithful. She misunderstood the reason for the stop.

"Let's not stop, Mike. Call me sentimental but I don't want to see Old Faithful until we're married."

"Then you'd better see it now because that isn't going to happen. We might as well have it out here and now with the car parked because I don't want to hit and be hit while I'm driving."

"Is this about Herbert Adams?" she asked angrily.

"No, it's about a two-timing little whore that jumped in bed with someone else three days after I left to do her dirty work in Las Vegas. As for her version and Harriet Smith's version of what went on Saturday night after the champagne was gone, I'll take Harriet's every time."

"All right, so I slept with him, it was your fault," she yelled back.

"And just how was it my fault that you took grandpa to

bed?"

"Will you just listen without interrupting me?"

"Yes."

"After you left on Wednesday I started to cry. I had nothing. No you, no car, no jewelry, no clothes, no money, not even a job. What if you didn't come back? In Las Vegas I had everything. How far I had fallen in six months. Then the landlord came by and wanted the rent and I didn't have it. I was about to be thrown out in the street, one of the homeless. I was scared. I invited him in and asked if he would like a cup of tea. He said that he would and when I put the cup in front of him my robe fell open. He almost dropped the tea trying to get a look. I told him that I wouldn't have the rent until Saturday and he took my hand and said he was sure we could work something out. I knew what he meant but I pretended that I didn't know what he was talking about and thanked him for his kindness. That's when the roses started coming and he asked me to go to the country club dance on Saturday. I told him I was busy because that was the day you were coming back, and I cleaned the house, bought lots of flowers for you and planned a great dinner with me for dessert. I even bought you a present.

"Your package came on Saturday with your hateful note. After I stopped crying I called Mr. Adams and asked if it was too late to accept his invitation, then I realized the banks were closed and I didn't know what to do with the bag full of money so I asked him to dinner and told him to bring a bottle of champagne. We had the champagne in front of the fire and when we finished he asked for my permission to court me. That was the word he used. I thought why not, he was loaded and the country club sounded good to me, even though everyone at Curly's laughed at it, and after a while I'd be a rich widow, so I served him your dinner and your dessert and I cursed you under my breath while he was on top of me for saying that you never wanted to see me again. We made a date for the hayride the next Wednesday and I told him to bring lots of blankets so no one could see what we were doing and he left a happy man. Was that so wrong, you prick?"

"Mary, is money that important to you?"

"Let me tell you about my childhood and how I grew up and you be the judge."

"You already did."

"That wasn't the truth. We were just getting acquainted and I didn't want to scare you away. Let me tell you about my real childhood."

She took a deep breath. There was no Bisbee, Arizona, or soccer or Girl Scouts, no high school plays or cheering the football team on. Bisbee, Arizona, had popped into her mind because that was where Kim Basinger was from in a movie she had seen and when she dyed her hair blonde she looked like her a little bit. Not Palm Beach either, as she said in Las Vegas. She was adopted as an infant and raised by John and Martha Defoe of Orange City, Florida, where her father sold Mary Carter paints. That was the first name that came to mind when she applied for a job at the Railroad Museum.

The Defoes had no children of their own and were very strict with her. She was plump when she was young and her schoolmates made fun of her and called her an Indian because of her shiny black hair but she grew and developed and by the time she was thirteen or fourteen she was conscious of how the boys looked at her. She loved the attention but her beauty angered her mother, who told her that beauty was a sign of the devil and a vain person. Her hair was cut short by her mother and her clothes were several sizes too big to hide from the world that she was becoming a woman.

Her father started to come to her room at night after she was in bed and they would pray that her beauty would leave her and that she would become plain again but she didn't mean it. He asked to see her breasts to see if the prayers were working and if they had stopped developing and she showed them to him. Each night he would feel them and tell her that they had to pray harder. She liked having him feel her breasts after the prayers were finished but she knew that her thoughts were sinful. He said that she must be fondling herself or her breasts wouldn't grow like that and she told him that she didn't do anything like that, although she knew that she did, which was a terrible sin, and she started to cry. He slapped her and said that he knew she was lying and that she was destined for Hell unless she told him the truth. When she admitted that she had touched herself he made her show him what she did and told her that he had to do something to her to save her soul and that it would hurt at first but then it would feel good and that would mean that their prayers were working.

She had heard about sex at school and no one had done it, but they described what they knew about it and she knew that was what she was doing with her father. When she told him what she had learned and that what they were doing was a sin outside of marriage he became furious and told her that her girlfriends were nothing but whores to talk like that, and that she would burn in Hell if she listened to them. He was a man of God, he said, who was trying to help her save her immortal soul and she was an ungrateful wretch to doubt him. She didn't really believe him and after that she didn't want to do it anymore, but he said it was part of the prayers and wouldn't stop, so she told her mother, who slapped her across the face and called her a lying whore and told her never to say such a thing again.

She got pregnant when she was sixteen. Both of them called her a whore and demanded to know who the father was. When she told them it was Daddy they hit her and called her a blasphemer and the whore of Babylon, which she didn't understand since she had never been out of the country.

THE CAPO'S MISTRESS

Martha said that her mother, whoever she was, was a whore for getting pregnant and she was doomed to follow in her mother's footsteps and there was nothing they could do to prevent it or save her soul, and that this was the thanks that they got for taking her in. She was thrown out of the house and told never to come back.

She went to a home for unwed mothers and after the baby was born she gave it up for adoption like her mother had done before her. When she heard it was a little girl she wept and would have prayed for her baby not to be placed with people like the Defoes if she believed in God anymore, but she didn't, or if there was a God she was sure he was a man and not to be trusted with her prayers.

She got a job as a waitress in Jacksonville and didn't finish high school or go back to Orange City. When she was eighteen she started seeing a man she met at the restaurant who told her he was single but his wife came to the restaurant and made a scene and she was fired. She went to Atlantic City and her looks got her a job in the chorus line. She couldn't sing or dance but the main part of the job was showing her tits and she had great ones. That was how she met Tony.

She soon discovered it was easy to make fools of men and that was what she did, what she was good at, how she took care of herself, and now that Tony was gone and she was getting old and ugly she didn't know what to do.

She concluded with, "The money in the bag will soon be gone, then I'll have to sell the jewelry and when that's gone I'll have to start selling myself. I don't know anything else."

Suddenly I felt sorry for her. I knew what she was going through. She was still beautiful but no longer young and her beauty was fading. She defined herself by her beauty and when it was gone she believed her life would be over, she would be just going through the motions, a conquest here and there, fewer and fewer, men no longer young, and men no longer interested in spending more than one night with her.

I decided it was time for me to come clean with Mary as she had just done with me. I started by telling her that I was a recovering alcoholic. Just like that, out of the blue.

She was taken aback. "But the wine and all those bottles you bought for our first dinner?"

"They were for you. I tried to just sip, or at least go slow. I wanted to get you in bed more than I wanted to get drunk. I hadn't had a drink for seven years, eight months and sixteen days until I went to Henry's Lake to visit Tom Faris just before I met you. He's why I started drinking in the first place, I know it now, and I honestly believe as long as I stay clear of him I'll be okay."

"Then why are we going to see him?" she asked.

"Because I need a backup for Sunday, then we're through with him."

"Who is he? All you've told me is that he's a great shot."

I told her about Five, how he became my partner when I got out of the Academy, that I signed false reports to cover for him when he beat some poor guy up, how he got his nickname, that he was on the take and so was I, and that it got to me so bad I started to hit the bottle.

"Why didn't you report him?"

"That's not the way I was brought up."

"What do you mean?"

"That the worst thing in the world is an informer. You don't rat out your partner, and the ads that tell kids to turn in their mother and father for smoking pot make me sick to my stomach. There was no way I was going to turn over Five and he knew it, but I also was an idealist, at least then, and I joined the force to make a difference, to put the bad guys away, and instead I became a bad guy myself. I couldn't understand what had happened to me. I hated myself. Then I became a drunk and a fat slob and I hated myself even more. It was only after

Five retired that I turned myself around and got a little self-respect back."

I thought about what I had just said and added, "Not very much self-respect. I hate myself for the things that I did and I always will."

"Do you hate Five?"

I thought for a while then answered, "Yes, I guess I do. I might have been a better person if it wasn't for him, but I did it to myself too. I know now that I should have turned him in but it's too late, I can't make a difference anymore, I'm washed up, I don't know what to do with the rest of my life. You were my only hope."

"But you *have* me for the rest of your life, silly, and with five million dollars think of the fun we'll have and the places we'll see."

She didn't get it and I didn't look at her as I said, "Mary, I'm not talking about money, I'm talking about self-respect. Do you think wearing Armani suits will make me feel better about myself when I look in the mirror? Gino has one of those but he's still a scumbag. By the way, did you sleep with him?"

I couldn't drive out of my mind the picture of Herbert Adams on top of her, that's why I asked the question, she had given him the dessert that was meant for me, but I regretted the question the minute it popped out. I didn't want to hear the answer.

"Yes, we had an affair," she said angrily, "but then I've slept with just about anyone you can name so there's nothing unusual about it. I'm addicted to sex, Mike, the same way you're addicted to liquor. When I see a good-looking man that's the first thing I think of. There, I've said it. Now you'll never marry me and I don't blame you."

She jumped from the car in tears and ran toward the geyser with me following. I grabbed her just as she got to Old

Faithful and turned her around and sat her down on one of the benches around the geyser as she struggled against me. There had been a snowfall last night and everything was white, the trees, the turrets of the lodge, the cars in the parking lot, the trail to the geyser and the benches where we sat. We were alone at the geyser in the snow. Overhead the sky was filled with white clouds and a black thunderhead lay against the distant mountains. The air smelled of wood smoke from the lodge and a wolf howled somewhere in the forest.

Mary stopped fighting and sat there gasping for air, exhausted by her struggle, each exhalation a white steaming plume in the cold air. She was still crying and the tears frosted her cheeks. I've never seen anything so beautiful. I turned her face to me and kissed her. She tried to push me away then stopped, her arms slipping around my neck.

When we broke I took her hand. "Mary, I still love you."

I was going to say more but my words brought back the words of Jeb on the tape. I still love her, he had said, and the sex was fantastic he had said, and she had dumped him when she found out that he couldn't swim because he was useless to her. She wanted me now because she couldn't get the five million dollars without me, but I would be gone like Jeb the minute she got the money in her money-grubbing little hands. She was still using me, twisting me around her finger with her lies. When the hell was she telling the truth and when wasn't she? I don't think even she knew. I started to get mad. I could feel it. I wanted to hit her. I wanted to kill her. My hands doubled into fists. I stood up and walked away from her, trying to control myself. She sat on the bench looking after me with a strange expression on her face. I suppose she was wondering what had happened. I had just kissed her and told her that I still loved her and she probably thought that she had it made, that I was back on the hook again, but now I was storming away with my fists doubled up. Why? I could see the question on her face.

I took a couple of deep breaths to get control of myself and walked back to her. She looked up at me.

"Go ahead and hit me. Beat the shit out of me. It will do us both good. That's what you want to do, isn't it?"

That stopped me cold. I looked at her, feeling suddenly foolish, and said, "Yes."

"Then do it. I deserve it. I've lied to you from the start. You were my last hope to get the goddamn bag out of the lagoon so I went to bed with you to get you interested in a hurry. You didn't have to buy all that wine, I was a sure thing. I wanted you to fall in love with me so I gave you a free sample of what was to come. I didn't love you. I just wanted you to go to Las Vegas for me. But a funny thing happened, Mike, I fell for you too. I could hardly wait for you to come back from Vegas and I thought it was because I wanted to get the money and my jewelry back, then the box came and I had them back and instead of being happy I started to cry. I had cleaned the house and bought steaks for dinner and loads of flowers to arrange. While I working I was thinking of what we would do after dinner, maybe on the table or in front of the fire, and I got so wet I had to change my panties. It was going to be a celebration. Everything looked so pretty. Then I read your mean letter and I started to cry and I realized it was you I wanted back, not the money or the jewelry, and I had lost you. I've been a fool. Go ahead and hit me. Beat the crap out of me. I deserve it and I want you to hit me."

She turned her face toward me, waiting for the blows to land, and I stood there in silence. Was she telling the truth? Of course she was, I said to myself, who could make up a story like that? She could, I shot back, how many times do you have to get taken before you wise up? You want to believe she loves you. She knows it and she's using that to get to you. She's going to break your heart again, it's as simple as that. Now wait a minute, I argued, suppose she is telling the truth and I let my one chance for happiness get away, I've got to take the chance. All right, sucker, I sighed, but don't say I didn't warn you.

I looked down at her waiting to be hit.

"Mary, stop it. I'm not going to hit you but I am going to be blunt. Tony told me I shouldn't trust you and I didn't believe him but now I do. I told you last night there would be no more lying or we were through. This morning I found out that you were still lying to me and you were sleeping with some old fart named Herbert Adams who was your backup retirement plan. I can forget about Adams but I can't forget about the lie, so I guess we're through."

She came off the bench and grabbed me around the knees.

"Please, Mike, please don't say that. I've never been in love in my whole rotten life. Please don't take it away from me now that I've found it. I'll be a good wife and I'll make you happy every day of your life, you'll see, and I'll never lie to you again."

"Mary, I want us to tell Bob Hill the truth and have him help us on Sunday. If we get something from the Feds for turning over Tony that's all to the good, if we don't that's the breaks, and I want to take the job as deputy sheriff and live in Virginia City with you as my wife for the rest of our lives. If you can handle that, say so. If not, then I guess it's all over between us, but don't lie to me."

She got to her feet and threw her arms around me.

"Oh, Mike, you won't be sorry. Let's go see Bob Hill and let's get married as soon as possible." She looked up at me with those incredible green eyes and I kissed her and pulled her close to me. I heard the roar and felt the ground tremble as Old Faithful erupted.

chapter eighteen

As we pulled back onto the main road from the Old Faithful turnout Mary asked if we could pick up her car at the airport in Billings, so I headed for the north entrance to Yellowstone Park toward U.S. 90.

"We're going to drive through some beautiful scenery," I told her. "I ran along this road with the running team. It's an amazing area and we might see a herd of elk or two."

She squeezed my arm and smiled. "Let's take it slow and enjoy it. Maybe we can stay overnight in Billings. I don't want to go to your partner's house at Henry's Lake, he's a terrible man, and I don't want to go back to the house in Virginia City right after the shooting. There may be a mess and it gives me the creeps to think about it. When you call Bob Hill would you ask if we can stay with him tomorrow night and go over everything then?"

"That doesn't give us much time," I said.

"Please, we can drive to Virginia City from Billings in the morning. I can't face the house yet. I promise I'll be nice to you in Billings."

She squeezed my arm and smiled at me and that was all it took.

We stopped at Fountain Paintpot and she was right, there was no reason to hurry with so much beauty and wonder to see. The paintpots are large springs filled with hot clay and vary in color from white to shades of pink and black. Fountain Paintpot is spectacular. I had run by it with the running team but didn't get a chance to stop and now I was glad we did. The snow at Old Faithful was here too but it was eerie to see it amid the steam from the paintpots. No one was around and we threw a few snowballs like a couple of kids and suddenly I felt great. I wasn't sure I trusted her yet but I was glad I was with her. I knew how I would have felt now if we walked away from each other back at Old Faithful.

We drove through the geyser basins and on to Mammoth Hot Springs with herds of elk and deer off in the distance against the trees. I did stop here with the running team and I was looking forward to seeing it again and showing it to Mary. The springs were created by limestone deposits and are massive terraces of white. They remind me of huge coral reefs without the ocean, if you can picture such a thing, and we wandered in awe among them.

We left the park through the north entrance and drove alongside the Yellowstone River for a while, at last coming to U.S. 90, where I turned east toward Billings, thinking this was the same route that I had taken a few days ago leading Tony's goons away from Virginia City and Mary. What a lot had happened since then.

"Are you hungry?" I asked her.

"Famished. Let's look for a cute place."

"Like Curly's," I laughed.

"At this point I don't care, I'm getting a headache. Don't you ever eat?"

"You said you were going to be nice to me."

"In Billings. We're not there yet."

We got off the interstate at Greycliff and found a steakhouse, which is pretty much all you can find in Montana. It wasn't cute and it wasn't Curly's but the food was okay.

When we had eaten I said, "Tell me about the country club. You said everyone at Curly's hated it. Why?"

"This isn't about Mr. Adams again, is it?"

I noticed she always called him Mr. Adams, like she hardly knew him, and I didn't want to kid her about it, so I just said no, that I was curious about the country club.

She said she had never been to the country club but it was a standing joke with the crowd that hung out at Curly's because not a single member was a cattleman. Most were land developers or land speculators like Herbert Adams and they came from L.A. or Silicon Valley or Seattle with lots of money, trying to get away from the life style that they had created there, parking lots and bumper-to-bumper traffic. They were engaged in bringing that lifestyle to Montana, at a profit, and they were joined in membership at the country club by those who served them, doctors, lawyers and tax accountants.

The country club was about thirty miles outside of town and featured three eighteen-hole golf courses, lots and lots of tennis courts, an Olympic-size outdoor pool which was drained in the winter, an indoor pool open year round, condominiums surrounding the golf courses selling at $500,000 and up, and a huge clubhouse with a chef stolen from a Beverly Hills restaurant who announced on arrival that he was bringing light cuisine to Montana. There was a shopping center adjacent to the country club with boutiques and a Starbucks so that its members would never have to come into town, and few of them did. She supposed that Mr. Adams lived in one of the condominiums and she made a point of saying that she had never seen it. She didn't know much about him except that he was buying up most of the property in Virginia City and it was rumored that he planned to bring in a Wal-Mart.

"Sounds a lot like L.A. or Las Vegas," I offered.

"It does," she replied, "and maybe the crowd at Curly's doesn't like the country club, but it sounds just fine to me. And what's the matter with a Wal-Mart? The people in Virginia City hate the idea but that's progress, and if I'm going to live there the rest of my life that's what I want, and a Starbucks and a boutique or two wouldn't hurt either."

She stopped and looked at me and I knew what was coming.

"Oh, Mike, do we have to live there? It's such a small town. You heard about Harriet Smith looking out her window all day to stick her nose into everyone else's business. They're all like that. When I told Sam we had a fight it was all over town the next minute and when I took back your gift the shopkeeper said he was expecting me because he heard we had a fight.

"I can't believe how much I've aged since Las Vegas. Only six months and I've got a wrinkle in my forehead that wasn't there before and lines around my eyes and the beginning of a double chin and when I tried to get some Botox the man thought it was something for cows. In Vegas I had a personal trainer, a masseuse and facial creams for everything. The only thing they have in Virginia City is cold cream. I look in the mirror and I'm falling apart. All they think about in town is cows and horses and the way it was there in the Civil War. Who cares?

"Could we please live at the country club and learn to play golf? We've got the $250,000 for a deposit on a condo. I don't want to set foot in that house again. It's a hundred years old. I want something new where the plumbing works and you get heat by pressing a button. And air conditioning. You haven't spent the summer here yet. I can't stand another summer sitting in front of a fan with a wet towel draped over it. For God's sake, this is the twenty-first century, not frontier days. What's the matter with these people?"

I hated to break the news to her but I did. "Mary, the $250,000 isn't ours. It's skim money. It's the first thing the government will grab and then the Capri and the feds will fight over how it's cut up."

She was stunned. "What? That's my money. I'm not going to turn it over to anyone."

I was about to go over it again when I saw the squad cars pull up outside—three of them with two officers each. Someone in the restaurant had made us from the newspaper photos and called the cops.

They took us to the station in cuffs and only then did they call Bob Hill as I had asked them to do in the restaurant. He straightened it out and I was allowed to talk with him and told him that we had to see him and asked if we could stay with him Saturday night after we had picked up Mary's car. He said to drop by in the afternoon and explained that he had cancelled the all-points but he couldn't do anything about our pictures in the papers. One of the cops got on the phone to tell him that we said we were headed for the airport in Billings and he thought it was a mistake to let us go and they had a spat about jurisdiction right there in front of us. Bob Hill finally won out but no one was very friendly as we walked out of the station. My copper-stopper didn't help at all. I think the words Los Angeles and California got them particularly upset and one of them asked if I was a friend of Jane Fonda. I said that I had a previous relationship with her and didn't want to discuss it in front of my wife-to-be because she was very jealous.

"You never told me about Jane Fonda," Mary said, for the cop to hear, "was she better in bed than me?"

The cop looked at Mary, then at me, and shook his head.

Richard Harris

"You ought to come to California," I said to him as I walked out of the station.

chapter nineteen

Mary tied a scarf around her head to hide her blonde hair. We decided to drive through Billings and stay at a hotel near the airport and Mary excused herself to get some black hair dye while I called Five to tell him we would meet him in Old Town on Sunday instead of staying overnight at his place.

"Kiss your blonde goodbye," Mary said when she came back to the room loaded down with packages.

I asked what was in them and she said it was a surprise and I would have to wait. "I'm going in the bathroom and when I come out you'll have a brunette on your hands. I said I'd be nice to you, remember?"

"I'm going to miss the blonde. Can I make love to her before she goes? For old time's sake?"

She kissed me lightly on the cheek. "The brunette will make you forget all about her."

Mary came out of the bathroom and she was right, I forgot all about the blonde. She stood there in one of those short nightgowns that has a fancy French name—perignon, I think, or maybe that's a champagne. She spun around.

"Surprise. How do you like it?"

How do I like it, I thought, does a dog like a bone? I wanted to rip the thing off her and throw her on the bed. It was emerald green satin to match her eyes, held up by two narrow green straps, and she wore emerald green slippers. As she spun around it flared out and up like those costumes ice skaters wear, except that Mary didn't have anything on underneath. She looked different with black hair the color of a moonless night, more predator than woman. Her green eyes were those of a black panther, beautiful but dangerous. Her hair spilled down onto her shoulders and did a dance of its own, the dance of Salomé, tempting, erotic, something that her blonde hair could never do. You could take the blonde home to meet your mother. The old girl would be shocked but you could get away with it. She looks a little fast, she would say to herself, but if they love each other maybe it will work out. Not with this one. Your mother would take you to one side and tell you that this was not the girl for you. She's beautiful but there's something about her that's too wild, too sensual, that's the word, all her prim and proper manners can't fool me, you'll never be able to tame her, domesticate her, I'll bet she can't even boil water. Then before she could stop herself a fleeting thought of what it would be like to be her, to be that beautiful animal completely without morals, would cross her mind and she would color and drive the thought away.

Mary came toward me slowly, everything moving. I was obviously in heat but she wanted to tease. She put a pout on her lovely face. "You don't like it."

I hadn't answered her first question because I couldn't get my breath and she knew it, but now I was going to suffer in agony until she had her fun.

"I love it."

That didn't satisfy her and the pout stayed on. "Then you

don't like me as a brunette."

"I love you as a brunette," I answered brilliantly.

The pout lessened. "Are you sure? I went to so much trouble picking this out. I'll bet you didn't even notice that it matches my eyes."

"It was the second thing that I noticed."

She was curious. "What was the first?"

"That the hair between your legs matched the hair on your head for a change. I got a pretty good view."

"Men. You're all alike."

"I thought you were a virgin."

The pout left her face and she smiled at me, a dazzling smile framed by her jet black hair. She moved toward me again until she was at the bed. She touched the two straps on her shoulders as only women can do, a man would have fumbled forever in that unfamiliar territory, and the gown fell away. She stood there.

"Let's pretend it's the first time for the both of us."

I took the cue.

"I've never done this before so I may be awkward."

"Neither have I. Please be gentle with me."

"We'll have to teach each other," I said as I pulled back the covers.

She climbed timidly into bed beside me and started to cry.

I sat up. "What's the matter? What did I do wrong?"

"I wish it was true," she said between sobs. "I wish it was the first time for the both of us and we could start all over. I don't want to be with anyone but you, ever."

I took her in my arms. "And I don't want to be with anyone but you. We can start over."

We lay back on the soft mattress and rolled into each other.

She giggled. "What do we do next?"

"Let me try this."

She moaned. "Oh, it feels wonderful. No wonder everyone talks about it."

"I don't think they talk while they're doing it."

"Oh," she said, and didn't say another word.

That night I had a nightmare. I was in a coffin and Mary was beside me. The coffin was metal and glass and filled with money and I could see the sides of the grave rising up around us to daylight at the top. Tony and his thugs and Five and Sam Culpepper and Jeb Breckenridge were looking down at us. Sam Culpepper was trying to deliver a eulogy but when he spoke the others laughed at him and threw dirt down on us. Sam said we were a new legend of Virginia City, better than the Civil War and better than Jack Dempsey and Doc Kearns, because those things happened a long time ago and he knew us and could tell anyone who wanted to listen about how we fell in love in Virginia City and how we were hunted down by Big Tony Danzante, who was insanely jealous of Mary, although he called her Theresa. The others broke up laughing after Sam's eulogy and started to throw dirt down on us in earnest. I tried to yell at them to stop but no sound would come, so I tried to pound on the glass top of the coffin but I couldn't raise my arms. Mary turned and looked at me from a face that was burned beyond recognition. She had no eyes. "Kiss me," she said. I screamed and sat bolt upright in bed. I was drenched in my own sweat. Mary woke and grabbed me.

"Mike, Mike, what's the matter?" I recoiled in horror at her touch.

"Turn on the light," I screamed. The light came on but I couldn't look at her. The nightmare was too real. She would have no face, no eyes, I knew it, I was sure of it. She took me in her arms.

"Mike, you've had a bad dream. It's all right now." She held me tight and I finally opened my eyes. She was as beautiful as ever.

"Mary, thank God you're okay. It was horrible."

"What was it about?"

"I don't want to talk about it. Maybe in the morning. Go back to sleep."

She rolled over and in a minute she was asleep and I was next to her with my eyes wide open. I never wanted to have that dream again.

Early in the morning the sun illuminated the cheap drapes and I fell asleep for the first time since the nightmare. About an hour later Mary woke me.

"I want to hear about your dream. You scared me to death last night."

"I can't remember it all but we were in a coffin together and it was full of money. I could see the sides of the grave rising up around us. I think I was seeing this damn mattress. Tony and his gang were throwing dirt on us. I couldn't wake up and I tried to scream but nothing would come. Then you turned your face toward me and it was burned away and you didn't have any eyes. That's when you heard me screaming."

"Oh, that's horrible. Try to forget about it."

"I didn't fall asleep until about an hour ago. I was afraid I would have the dream again."

She kissed me and put her leg over me and slowly the remaining images of the nightmare melted away.

We showered and Mary started hot water in a little coffee pot that was in the room with a tray of instant coffee. I went downstairs and brought up some stale coffeecake that was on a plate on the front desk and that was breakfast. Mary didn't seem to mind but maybe she was being nice.

She smiled at me and took a sip of coffee, then turned on the pout. "What about when we're in Curly's and all those sweet young things wiggle by you? Wouldn't you rather be with one of them?"

"No, and you don't like the people at Curly's so we won't go there anymore."

She feigned surprise. "How can you say that if we're going to live in that cute little house that you're going to build a white picket fence around? The deputy sheriff has to take his beautiful wife out to dinner and dancing at Curly's at least once a week. It's right down the street."

I was blindsided. "What are you talking about? You hate Virginia City."

"Not if you're there. You're going to be the deputy sheriff and I'm going to be so proud of you I wouldn't live anywhere else."

"What about golf at the country club and France and Spain and all those other places you wanted to see?"

"That's for people who are bored with their lives. I've seen them in Las Vegas running from one show to the next or one casino to the next or one restaurant to the next for something to tell their friends about when they get home. In Europe you run from one cathedral to the next or one museum to the next but it's the same idea. I want to settle down and learn to cook something besides steak and baked potatoes. Did you know that's all I know how to do?"

I looked at her, that's all I could do. Lovesick, I know it was written all over my face. I wished I could tell her how I felt, so proud of her, but all that would come out was, "Mary." I kept saying it over and over. I reached out and touched her hair.

"I know," she said, touching my face with her hand, "I love you too. Isn't it wonderful?"

When we got to the airport I couldn't find Mary's car. I remembered parking it and running for the terminal to catch the flight to Minneapolis/St. Paul but I forgot to make a note of where I left the car. We drove up and down each aisle until at last Mary spotted it. I parked in back of the Mercedes and took the bug off the rear license plate and showed it to Mary. I didn't know if it was still working or, if it was, whether anyone was monitoring the signal in Las Vegas, but I couldn't take any chances. I put the bug on the rear license plate of a police car parked a few stalls down. As I did so I said a prayer that the bug was still working and that someone would spot the moving signal and report it to Bill Accardo. I knew he wanted to make points with Tony.

"It's been sitting here in the snow for quite a while," I said as I handed the keys to Mary. "We'd better see if it starts before I drive away."

Mary got behind the wheel and I climbed into the passenger seat. I looked around. Something was bothering me. Mary put the key in the ignition and started to turn it. I grabbed her hand. The dream, it was like the dream. We were in a glass and metal coffin.

"Take the key out, quick," I yelled at her, and she almost jumped through the roof. "The car's been booby-trapped. I know it."

Her eyes went wide with fear. She got the key out of the ignition and I took it from her.

"Now get out of the car and hide behind my car," I ordered.

When she was behind my car I looked for the hood release. I was just a dumb cop on the L.A.P.D. and I had never worked on the bomb squad. I didn't know what to do. Was it safe to pull the hood release? I sat there. The bomb would go off when the car was started, which really had nothing to do with opening the hood, so I took a deep breath and pulled the release. There was a smooth sound of the hood opening and that was all. I was still alive.

I got out of the Mercedes and raised the hood and looked for the bomb. What the hell would it look like? Everything seemed okay to me. I slid under the car on the wet snow and looked up through the open hood. I still could see nothing out of the ordinary.

I climbed back into the driver's seat and put the key back in the ignition. There was only one way to find out if the car was wired and that was to start it. I hadn't been a very good Catholic, in fact I had been a lousy Catholic, but that was still my religion, so I said the Act of Contrition.

I asked myself, would this work? I was thinking about heaven and the Act of Contrition, not the bomb. It seemed so unfair. I had just had a great night in the sack, one of many with Mary, and I hadn't been to confession in over twenty years. My confession would probably make St. Augustine blush and yet I was asking God to punch my ticket for the Pearly Gates. What about the poor guy who had lived a good life but had a heart attack in the middle of beating off? Straight down to Hell. I would pass by him on my way up to Heaven and wave.

"Too bad you didn't have time for an Act of Contrition," I would yell over to him and he would give me the finger and scream horribly as he plunged into eternal hell-fire.

I turned the key. The engine started without a hitch and purred smoothly. No bomb. I got out of the Mercedes and walked back to where Mary was hiding behind my car. I looked at her sheepishly.

"Your car is waiting, madam," I said. "It was the dream. I thought about the metal and glass coffin the minute I sat in your car and I knew it had been rigged by Tony to blow up when it was started. It was like an omen. Sorry."

She laughed with relief and at me and it was okay.

She got in the Mercedes and I started my car and we left the airport together for the sheriff's house, but the big red Mercedes soon left the old clunker in its dust and I was left alone with my thoughts. I was happy, I was content, I was goofy in love, then the voice started in on me. Wake up, dummy, she's got you wrapped around her little finger again, right where she wants you, have a little backbone for a change. You told her one more lie and that was it, the finish, washed up, done, over with. Well, she went right ahead and lied to you and you caught her at it and for some reason I can't figure out you're happy as a new puppy with a bone. Remember what Tony said, don't trust her. He should know, he's in a wheelchair. For Christ's sake, what more do you want? Look, I answered, I'm going to lay it out to you even though you know everything I'm going to say, you dumb fuck, and this shouldn't be necessary. I love the woman. She just told me that she loves me and wants to get married and live in our little house in Virginia City where I'll be the deputy sheriff and she'll be waiting when I come home. What am I supposed to say to her, that she's a lying bitch? I've got no choice but to believe her until she proves me wrong. Now shut up and leave me alone.

I spent the drive enjoying the scenery and thinking what a beautiful place this was to live and how lucky I was to be here with my life laid out before me, no more doubts or regrets, each day looking forward to getting up and doing my job and coming home at night to my wonderful wife, and maybe, just maybe, we could have children, we're not too old yet, a girl for Mary and a boy for me.

I went too far. The voice could keep quiet no longer: Children, what a laugh, she's worried about wrinkles and you want to give her stretch marks. No way, do you seriously think she would agree to that?

Why not? She wants to learn how to cook and keep house. Children will be the next thing she'll want, wait and see, that's how women think when they finally settle down. You're really good, came the reply, where did you get your degree in female psychology? Okay, okay, I can do without the sarcasm, I told you once to shut up and leave me alone and I meant it.

I drove the rest of the way in peace and got to Bob Hill's

place about four in the afternoon and expected to see Mary's car in front of the house but it wasn't there.

chapter twenty

Sheriff Bob Hill had a forty-acre spread along the Madison River near Cameron, about ten miles before the turnoff for Virginia City. It was just a few miles from the spot where my car broke down, and I must have passed right by it coming back from Five's place. He met me at the door.

"Where's Mary?"

"I don't know. She picked up her car at the airport in Billings and left me in her dust. I thought she would be here waiting for me. I hope nothing's happened to her. I didn't see her car along the way."

I sounded worried and I was. The sheriff picked up on it.

"Come on in and have a drink. It's still early. Maybe she stopped to get something to eat. That's a long drive."

He introduced me to his wife, Thelma, and she said we were invited for dinner and hoped that we liked pot roast. She went back into the kitchen and Bob poured us both scotches and water.

When we were seated he opened with our arrest in Greycliff and said he wanted me to know that he had cancelled the all-points and was sorry for the inconvenience. I told him to forget it and we looked around for another subject. I could tell he was worried about Mary, and so was I, but neither of us brought it up. An hour or more passed with small talk and then the phone rang. It was Mary.

She took the wrong turnoff, then had car trouble, and Jeb had towed her to Sam's garage. It was closed and Sam wasn't around so she was going to leave the car and Jeb would drive her to the sheriff's house. She would be there in about half an hour. I told Bob Hill and he said he would have Thelma wait dinner.

When Mary finally got there Bob did a double-take on Mary's black hair.

"I didn't want us to get picked up by the police again," she stammered as Bob introduced her to Thelma, who was not very friendly once she got a look at Mary, or maybe it was because she had been holding dinner for her.

"I've heard a lot about you," was all she could manage, and of course she had.

We apologized for barging in the way we had and thanked them for their hospitality and things got friendlier after a few glasses of wine. Mary wanted to know how to make such a delicious pot roast and said all she could cook was steak and baked potatoes and she was afraid I would get tired of it. Thelma thawed and gave her the recipe and then Mary and Thelma did the dishes together and we were just folks. After the dishes were put away the sheriff asked Thelma to excuse us and we went into his office, which was furnished Montana lawman style with heads of elk and deer on the walls alongside an old fashioned gun rack filled with antique guns. He sat behind a big oak desk and we took two cowhide-covered chairs in front.

I looked at Mary. "Do you want to tell him what this is all

about or shall I?"

Mary looked defeated. "Go ahead."

I gave it to the sheriff as best I could remember it, including my conversation with Tony and the exchange set for noon tomorrow, and Mary helped me from time to time. When I had finished all Sheriff Hill could say was, "Whew, what a mess. We don't have much time."

"No," I agreed.

"I don't want to call the F.B.I. All they'll do is throw their weight around and mess things up. What do you think?" he asked.

"A bunch of klutzes."

I knew a Montana lawman would agree with that statement and the sheriff did.

"Is your backup man good?" he asked.

"He's a good shot, if that's what you mean, but I promised him $100,000 out of the five million. He may back out when I tell him there's no payday."

Mary turned to me. "I thought we agreed on fifty and that we weren't going to have any secrets anymore."

"What difference does it make whether it's fifty or a hundred?" I replied, ducking the question about secrets from each other. "Now he's not going to get anything."

"I wouldn't say that," Bob said. "You may be in line for a whistleblower's fee. He can get part of that. If he doesn't want in, I can act as your backup, these guys are from Las Vegas and they won't know me."

I nodded. "That might work, but remember, there's only supposed to be me and a backup. If Tom Faris agrees to stay in, you have to stay out of sight; otherwise they'll get spooked and maybe start shooting."

"I'd like to have more people in reserve if anything goes wrong. The problem is I'm holding down the fort alone. I told you I needed another deputy and the deputy I have is on vacation in Hawaii. It's nine o'clock Saturday night. This whole thing goes down in fifteen hours. We don't have enough time to get help. Do you think we can handle it alone?"

"Look," I said, "there doesn't have to be any shooting. Let the exchange go through but put a wire on me and set up a camera to film the action. I'll get them to implicate Tony and we've got the whole thing on the record. When the exchange goes through either my partner or you and I will draw down on them and you can arrest them for the murder of Herbert Adams. They'll go right to the slammer without bail and we'll have the ledger, the five million dollars and a record of what went down. The U.S. Attorney may not even need Mary as a witness. We can wrap the whole case up tomorrow and I think we can do it by ourselves." I sounded more confident than I was.

"Where will I be if your partner stays in?" the sheriff asked, and I noticed he was letting me run the show. The job as deputy sheriff was as good as mine.

"You stay with the camera and the tape recorder and make sure we get everything down, then come out and make the arrest. Let's get out there early and set up."

"I'm going with you," Mary said.

"No, you're not, it's too dangerous," I replied.

"Do you realize that there are women in the armed forces in Iraq right now? You just don't get it, do you? I can handle myself. When I want your protection I'll ask for it."

She turned to the sheriff. "Have you ever had a woman deputy, Bob?"

He looked embarrassed. "No, but I'm thinking about it."

"Well, think about this, both of you. I'm the only one who knows where the ledger is, so you pretty well have to take me."

"Mary, be reasonable," I heard myself saying. How original, that's what I said yesterday and the day before.

"Mike, I'm coming along tomorrow or you won't get the ledger. I've gone through too much, given up too much, not to be there at the end." She looked directly at me, daring me to try to talk her out of it, but I simply said okay.

We left the sheriff's office and Thelma showed us to our room. When we were alone I asked what had happened to her car.

"Jeb said he thought it was something to do with the distributor, whatever that is."

I knew I shouldn't go there, that it would cause trouble, but I couldn't help it, suspicion and the green-eyed monster had me in their grip.

"How was Jeb?"

"Fine," she replied, with an edge in her voice as she said it.

"Did he make a pass at you?"

"No."

"You're not very communicative," I said. "What did you talk about?"

She turned and looked straight at me.

"What a suspicious prick you are, and that you would be sure to grill me about him the minute you had a chance. Look, my car broke down. It happens. I didn't have a clue what was wrong and I called for a tow truck. Jeb answered the call. What a break for me. Do you want to know if we made love?"

That was exactly what I wanted to know and she knew it.

"No," I said, "I know you didn't do anything like that."

"Then why the hell are we having this conversation? I told you I loved you and that I wanted to marry you. Isn't that enough for you?"

I thought of the husband and wife having a fight at the lagoon at the Treasure Island in Las Vegas because he gambled past his limit and how I knew that he was going to lose big time. How do women do it? They've got a natural gift for argument and they love to win and will do and say almost anything to get the best of you. They should all be lawyers.

It was, in my opinion, perfectly normal to ask about Jeb. The facts are that she slept with him, that he said the sex was fantastic, that he said he was still in love with her, and that he would be in my position right now if the poor slob had learned how to swim when he was a kid. Under those circumstances, what man wouldn't ask questions if his beloved spent the afternoon in the company of Jeb, inside or out of a tow truck? I had every right in the world to be suspicious, and she knew it, so she took the offensive and made a stammering fool of me.

"Well," she said, in a tone that meant she wanted an answer to her question.

What was the question? I wondered. I had spent so much time feeling sorry for myself that I had forgotten what she had asked. I gambled.

"Yes."

"Then let's get to sleep. I'm exhausted."

I had apparently answered the question correctly and we went to bed. I tried to fool around but Mary said we were guests and that we shouldn't mess up the sheets. My ex-wife used to say things like that. We were practically married. I rolled over and went to sleep.

chapter twenty-one

Thelma called us to breakfast: eggs, ham, sausage, grits with sausage gravy, and steaming black coffee served with a view of the Madison River, now gray and cold with a light snow coming down. Thelma smiled warmly as the compliments flowed her way and the food disappeared. I was having a second cup of coffee when the phone rang and Thelma answered it and handed it to Bob, saying, "It's your dispatcher."

He listened, then asked incredulously, "A gas station stick-up on Sunday morning? Is anyone hurt?" He waited for the answer and then said, "A shooting? Have the paramedics been called?" He listened some more, then said, "Okay, I'm on my way."

He turned to Thelma. "Sorry, honey, there's been a service station holdup in McAllister and someone's been shot. I've got to get over there. How about you two coming into the office with me while I put on my belt and gun?" he asked, looking at us.

We followed him into his office, both taken aback by the

news. When we were inside the office with the door closed he turned to us. "McAllister is a small town past the Virginia City turnoff. Why anyone would want to stick up a gas station there on Sunday morning is beyond me, but somebody did and the attendant shot back. Most everybody in Montana has a gun and knows how to use it. Anyway, I've got to go. I hope you understand, I don't have a deputy I can send."

We said we did and I asked if he thought he would get back to Virginia City before noon.

"McAllister is about twenty-five miles from Virginia City, and this should take less than two hours. It depends on the roads in this weather. It'll be close but I should be there before noon."

He showed us the tape recorder and the camera and asked, "Do you know how to put a wire on, Mike?" I said that I did and asked where we should set up so he could find us.

Mary spoke up. "The Green Front Hotel is about as good a spot as I can think of. It has an unobstructed view of the Opera House. What do you think, Bob?" He agreed and we asked what we should do if he wasn't there by noon.

"If Mike's partner backs out because of the money I don't think you should try to do the exchange without me. Just hide in the hotel and don't show your faces. If he stays in then it's up to you. You were going to do it without me in the first place so I think you should decide." He reached in his desk and pulled out a manila envelope, then said, "I better get going, the faster I leave the better my chance of meeting you before noon. Good luck." We shook hands and he walked out of the office.

I gathered up the wire equipment and the camera and tripod, making sure the camera had film in it, and loaded everything in the clunker. We said our goodbyes to Thelma and headed for Virginia City. The roads were slippery and wet with snow that would turn into ice that night.

"I don't think Bob's going to be able to make it back before noon in this weather," I said to Mary. She nodded in agreement as we looked over the scene of the exchange. I got my service automatic out of the glove compartment of the clunker and shoved it in my belt.

"Let's go ahead and set up in the Green Front Hotel," Mary suggested. "It has a great view of the Opera House and it's far enough away so I won't be spotted. You'll have to show me how to put a wire on you."

I asked if she knew whether there was an alarm on the Green Front, figuring I would have to jimmy the door. She showed me a window in back that she said kids climbed in to make out in the old hotel, and I wondered how she happened to know about it but kept my mouth shut.

I pushed all the equipment through, then climbed in myself and helped Mary in. We set up the camera with a good view of the Opera House from the lobby window of the Green Front, and I disabled the alarm and broke the lock on the front door. Next came the wire and I showed Mary how to put it on me and operate the tape recorder.

When we were finished I turned to Mary. "Okay, where's the account book?"

"Right behind you," she said.

I turned and saw an office with a fake 1863 calendar on the wall, a roll-top desk and a big old railroad safe with a picture of a train on it and a bunch of dusty books in it.

"Where?"

"It's right in front of you," she said, laughing at my stupidity.

"Not one of those old books sitting there in the safe for everyone to see?" I asked.

"Where else but the safe would you put an account book? It wouldn't fit in the safe deposit box at the bank where I put the money and the jewelry, so I put it here. It looks like just another old book."

She beamed proudly and I complimented her, then walked over to the safe and took the top ledger off the pile. Sure enough, it was the book I pulled out of the sack in my room in Vegas, dripping water all over the carpet. That seemed so long ago now. We sat down to wait for Five.

I saw him coming from the lobby window of the Green Front and looked at my watch. It was twenty minutes after eleven. "Here he is," I said to Mary, and went outside to call him. We came back in together and I introduced him to Mary. He put down his rifle to shake hands with her.

"Pleased to meet you," he said.

"Tom, we've got to talk with you," I said. "There's been a change in plans."

"What's the change?" he asked, eyeing me suspiciously.

"We've gone to the sheriff, he should be here any minute," I answered, unsure how Five would take it. "We're going to turn in the money and the ledger we have and bring the whole mob down, how do you like that?"

Five's eyes narrowed. "Not very much. Since when did you become a Boy Scout?"

I remembered all the times I wanted to stand up to Five and didn't. This wasn't going to be one of them.

"It's the right thing to do, Tom."

"Why the hell didn't you call me so I could have stayed home?"

"We need your help."

"I don't work for free, where's my hundred thousand dollars coming from?"

"Tony skimmed over fifty million dollars from the Capri and we could get up to 10% for reporting it. We'll pay you out of that," I said, hating the wheedling sound in my voice.

"I was counting on the hundred thousand dollars, Mike. I knew it was too good to be true and it wasn't. I never got a break before so why should things be different now? I'm too old to ever see a dime of the reward money even if you get lucky and the feds give you something when it's all over."

He looked down at the floor as Mary and I waited for his answer. If Five took off and the sheriff wasn't here by noon, we'd have to hide in the hotel and hope they didn't find us. We'd be overmatched, and while I might tackle them if I was alone, I couldn't do it with Mary here. If they found us in the hotel we'd put up a hell of a fight and hope that the sheriff got here in time to save us. I couldn't let them take Mary alive and have Tony do to her what I thought he would do for making him a paraplegic, but I didn't want to think about that and drove the thought from my mind.

Five still didn't answer so I asked him, "How about it, Tom, for old time's sake?"

He looked at me with his strange expressionless eyes that always gave me the creeps when we were partners. "For old times' sake? Why not?"

Mary and I let our breath out and I showed him the wire I was wearing and the camera all set up on its tripod ready to roll.

"When the sheriff gets here he'll wait with Mary. I'm going to try to get them to say something about Tony while I count the money. As soon as I finish counting the money and say 'It's all here,' we'll both cover them and the sheriff will come out and arrest them for the murder of Herbert Adams, that's the guy you read about in the papers."

"What if the sheriff doesn't show up? It's getting close to noon. Where is he?"

"He got called to a filling station stick-up early this morning. He said he should be able to get back here before noon. If he's not here I figure we'll go it alone and make a citizen's arrest."

"Same old Mike."

We waited for Bob Hill. Waiting is always the hardest part for me, and I felt a drop of sweat trickle down my side although it was close to freezing in the unheated hotel.

I sat next to Five listening to him mutter to himself. He looked terrible. Maybe it was his dog getting shot or maybe it was losing out on the hundred thousand he was counting on.

"Tony Danzante," he mumbled, "that lousy son of a bitch has spent his whole life breaking the law and I've spent my whole life upholding it, but he has all the money and I don't have a pot to piss in. He can hand Mike and the broad five million dollars just like that and not miss it. Nobody knows how much he's got stashed away, the lousy scum bag. I wish I could take my rifle and shove it up his ass and pull the trigger. I'd like that. All his fucking money wouldn't save him then. I'd watch him die slow and listen to him beg me for help. I'd sip a beer until it was over, then I'd piss on him and walk away. I'd like that."

I watched him clench his jaw as he pictured Tony writhing on the floor, a bullet up his ass. A little bit of drool ran down his face as he gritted his teeth and said loudly, "God, I'd like to do that. I'd give anything to do that." Then he slumped back in his chair and was quiet.

When it was almost noon I walked to the lobby window. A car was pulling up next to Five's truck. I sighed in relief and my breath clouded the window. That's cutting it awfully close but it's better than Bob not being here at all, I thought. The car and Five's truck were at the far end of the pedestrian mall of Old Town and I didn't notice that it wasn't a police car.

Two men dressed in suits got out of the car. They looked around to get their bearings and started down the pedestrian street toward the Opera House. My heart sank; it wasn't Bob. It was Gino and Frankie here to do the exchange.

I turned around and looked at Five and Mary. "Tony's men are here. We'll have to go without the sheriff. We were going to do it without the sheriff anyway and keep the money, so nothing's changed."

Mary said, "It has, Mike, you weren't going to try to arrest them, that's what's different. They're not going to just surrender, not those two, there will be a gunfight, I know it. Let them go with the book. We'll have the five million dollars."

"And let them keep the ledger? No way. There's no case and no reward without the ledger, right, Tom?"

Five looked at Mary. "That's pretty much the way that it is, and I'm not doing this for my health."

I looked out the lobby window of the hotel. The two men were almost at the Opera House. One of them looked at his watch and I did the same. It was 11:59. Mary followed my gaze out the window.

"It's Gino and Frankie," she said.

"I know," I answered. "It's time to go. Give me a kiss for luck and start the tape recorder."

chapter twenty-two

    I stuck my automatic in my belt behind me and then picked up the ledger. Five cradled his rifle in one arm and we walked out the door to meet them. I looked around. The Railroad Museum was across the street, and I remembered turning around in front of it and pretending that I was just arriving in Virginia City heading for the Green Front Hotel.
    My first day in town. Well, I was an old timer now, headed down the main street of Old Town to meet two tough hombres. I looked at the old buildings. No one was in sight except the two mugs coming toward us, and a light, cold rain was falling. I had the feeling again that the citizens of Virginia City were inside the old buildings looking out at us, afraid to come out until it was all over, and maybe they were, only these citizens were long dead and only their ghosts inhabited Old Town. We stopped about five feet apart. I approached Gino with the ledger and held it out to him and he handed me a canvas bag that felt heavy with money. He opened the ledger and I opened the bag. I reached into the bag and flipped through a rubber-

banded stack of hundred dollar bills, one of many. The first few on the top and bottom were okay but the rest was cut paper. No wonder Tony said that getting five million dollars on short notice was no problem. We were being set up. Gino and Frankie were going to kill us.

"How's Tony?" I asked Gino as I pretended to look inside the bag and count the money with one hand while I tried to reach the gun in my belt with the other. Gino looked up from the ledger and smiled a dirty smile at me, like a cat playing with a mouse. He would have his fun and then strike.

"Tony? I don't know any Tony, do you, Frankie?"

"I don't think so. Let me think." He scratched his head. "Yeah, I know one, Tony Spumoni, the ice cream guy."

They were convulsed with laughter when Five said suddenly, "Which one of you greasy bastards shot my dog?"

Gino stopped laughing and looked straight at Five. "I did."

"Why?"

He winked at Frankie before he answered, then said, "I can't stand a barking dog."

Frankie started to laugh and then he heard the blast of Five's rifle and saw a red hole appear between Gino's eyes before his head exploded. Five was using dum-dums. Frankie clawed frantically for his gun and Five calmly watched him find it and start to raise it before he fired again and there was a red hole between Frankie's eyes.

Five covered me with the rifle and took my gun and the bag full of money.

"Sorry I've got to do this, Mike, but I know you'd chase after me even without a gun and I don't want to kill you, just slow you down."

He fired and I felt the high-powered slug tear into my thigh. It missed the bone, but the exit wound for the dum-dum took a big chunk of me with it, and I watched my blood mix with the sand of the square. Five bent down and removed the ledger from Gino's hand.

"I get the money and you get the girl, seems fair to me," Five said.

I grimaced at him, the pain was already starting. "I didn't want the goddamn money in the first place."

"I never could figure that out about you, Mike, you never thanked me for any of the stuff I cut you in on. You always had a chip on your shoulder when I gave you your share of the take, like you didn't want it."

I heard a noise and thought it was the pain throbbing through my body. I pulled off my belt and used it as a tourniquet to stop the flow of blood from my leg.

"I didn't want it but I didn't have the guts to turn you in so I took it. Why the hell would I thank you for making me sick to my stomach every time I looked in the mirror?"

The noise was louder now and we both recognized the sound so familiar in L.A., a police helicopter. I spotted it about a mile away and closing fast. I looked back at Five.

"It's the sheriff, Tom. You'd better kill me, you cold-blooded bastard, because I'm going to testify that I saw you shoot two men without warning. I hope you enjoy your money in hell."

"I wouldn't waste a bullet on you, you fucking drunk. Look me up on the Riviera, and if you kiss my ass I'll buy you a drink."

He took off running toward his truck carrying the bag full of money in one hand with his rifle and the account book in the other. He'll have a hard time paying for a drink on the Riviera with what's in *that* bag, I thought, and the thought took away some of the pain in my leg.

He got about ten steps before I heard the crack of a rifle behind me and Five fell in a heap. He had been hit in the leg and we both turned and looked back at the hotel, trying to find the shooter. A second shot missed and kicked up the sand next to Five and the flash gave away the shooter's location. A window of one of the second floor rooms was open and someone was steadying a rifle on the sill. The shooter had to be Jeb if he'd missed a shot like that. No surprise there, I thought, Mary crossed me. She was a lying bitch after all. I guess I knew it all along but didn't want to believe it. The voice inside me had the decency not to say I told you so, but now the pain came back into my leg worse than before.

Five saw the flash and started to raise his gun but a third shot caught him full in the chest before he could fire. His arms flew out and he dropped his rifle and fell on his back and didn't move.

A few seconds later the front door of the Green Front burst open and Mary and Jeb ran toward me. Jeb was carrying a rifle. I started to crawl toward Five's rifle but Jeb was on me before I could reach it and kicked me in the side, taking all of the wind out of me. I lay on the ground gasping for air. He drew back his boot to kick me again but Mary grabbed him.

"Don't, Jeb. Just get the money and the book so we can get out of here before the sheriff comes."

Mary turned to me as Jeb went to get the bag of money and the ledger.

"Sorry, Mike, it wasn't supposed to happen this way at all. We were going to take the money from you and your partner when you came back into the hotel. I couldn't give up the money, Mike. When it came right down to it I just couldn't do it. I didn't mean for you to get hurt. Please forgive me. You'll hear from me one day. I hope you'll come see me."

Jeb was already toast as far as Mary was concerned, the poor bastard. I didn't tell her that the bag was mostly full of cut paper. I could picture her face when she found out and I wished I could be there.

She turned and they started to run down the street in the

same direction Five had headed, directly toward the oncoming police helicopter, which started shooting at them without warning, no bull horn and no order to stop. They must do things different here in the Wild West, I thought, then I took another look at the helicopter, dead black and no markings, and I knew it was Tony as sure as I knew that my leg hurt like hell and that he was here to pick up Gino and Frankie and the ledger. I had to admire the plan, quick and daring, but he was in for a surprise.

A burst of automatic weapons fire from the helicopter tore up the board sidewalk in front of the Bale of Hay Saloon but Mary and Jeb were running along the sidewalk now, under the balconies and second floors of the old buildings that shaded it, and the shooter couldn't get a clear shot. A second burst smashed into the Sauerbier Blacksmith Shop and then the chopper was by them, Mary and Jeb running down the board sidewalk toward Five's truck and the helicopter passing over them in the opposite direction toward the Green Front Hotel.

I watched the helicopter make a pretty circle over the Green Front and head back into Old Town after them. I could see Lou and Tony as they passed by and Tony looked straight at me, as if to say, "You're next." I followed the helicopter as it headed back up the pedestrian street, to one side now to get a clear shot at the opposite sidewalk, and saw Mary and Jeb reach Five's truck and get in. Jeb disappeared for a second under the dash to hot wire the truck, and it roared to life and smashed through the wooden vehicle barrier onto the pedestrian street, empty of pedestrians, heading right for the helicopter. I realized that they were trying to pull the same stunt again, pass under the helicopter and deprive Tony of a clear shot, but even if it worked they would be sitting ducks when they reached the highway with no obstructions on either side. The truck drove up onto the sidewalk on the side of the street where the helicopter was passing and stayed close to the old buildings, taking out the supports for the second story balconies and roofs that shaded the sidewalk, and they fell in a heap in its wake. The bursts of automatic weapons fire went harmlessly over the truck and into the old buildings on the opposite side of the street and then the helicopter and truck were past each other again, going in opposite directions.

The truck sped by me and turned just before it hit the Green Front Hotel head on, skidding to a stop in a cloud of dust alongside. Jeb jumped out with his rifle and got between the truck and the hotel and I saw his plan, it was the only thing he could do, a man with a rifle versus men with a machine gun and helicopter, but you pick the spot for the fight, not them. The odds were still against him.

I watched the helicopter pull up and go wide, around the Green Front, and I thought they were leaving, but it turned and disappeared from view behind the hotel. They're going to land and take him on hand to hand, I thought, and Jeb must have had the same idea because he and Mary crawled under the truck. Suddenly the helicopter came out from behind the building with the machine gun firing into the space where Jeb had been, between the truck and the side of the building, chewing up the hotel and the truck, the windshield exploding into fragments, then it was by and heading up the street again.

Jeb rolled out from under the truck and steadied his rifle on the side of the truck bed, resting it there and peering through the sights. The helicopter made its graceful turn and headed back toward the hotel as Jeb drew a bead on the pilot.

According to the crowd at Curly's, Jeb was an average pool player and lousy at snooker. He had a nice even stroke with his cue and a lot of fancy shots, banks off the cushion and English on the ball, the whole bit, but he couldn't beat a good snooker player because he never thought about his position after his shot, so he never set himself up or snookered his opponent.

It reminded me of Five and the kid who had his finger shot off when he was standing behind it. I honestly believe that Five didn't intend to do any more than shoot off the offending finger, which was bad enough, but in the process he killed the kid, something he didn't intend to do. He just didn't think.

I could see what was going to happen now and I yelled to Jeb to let the helicopter go by and take out the pilot when it passed him, but he paid no attention to me. It was an easy shot and that was what he needed with the arm I had busted up for him. He pulled the trigger. As the helicopter bore down on the Green Front Hotel a hole appeared in its Plexiglas bubble.

Jeb saw the pilotless helicopter heading directly at the truck and him and realized too late the consequences of his shot. He yelled to Mary and they started to run. They would have made it with time to spare but Mary must have thought about the bag in the front seat with five million dollars in it. She stopped running and went back to the truck. She reached through the shattered front window to grab the bag of money on the seat and started to pull the bag through the broken window, but it caught on the jagged edges of the shattered safety glass and hung up. She pulled harder and I could see her look at the helicopter coming toward her at a hundred miles an hour. I yelled to her that the bag was worthless and was full of cut paper, but she couldn't hear me over the roar of the chopper on its collision course with the truck and the Green Front hotel.

The hole in the glass was almost big enough for the bag, but not quite, and she grabbed the glass with her bare hands and tried to break a piece off, her blood spurting through her fingers. The glass broke and she fell back against the side of the hotel with the bag in her hands as the helicopter struck the truck and drove it and Mary into the Green Front, splintering through the hundred-and-forty-year-old wood as if it wasn't there. The helicopter exploded in a ball of fire and the old building was engulfed, the flames shooting up the side of the hotel.

I thought at once of the nightmare, Mary's beautiful face burned away and sockets where her luminous green eyes used to be. A coffin full of money. It was a warning, an omen, and I had misread it in Billings at her car. It was money I had never wanted and that I should not have helped her get from Tony. It was a warning that if I did Mary would die horribly. I had ignored the nightmare and it was coming true before my eyes. I screamed, "No, no," and kept screaming as I tried to get to my feet. The tourniquet had made my injured leg numb from lack of blood. It wouldn't support me and I fell to the ground. I ripped the belt away and tried to stand but the blood supply hadn't yet returned and I fell again. I started to crawl to the hotel, leaving a trail of blood in the sand. I heard running footsteps behind me and turned my head. It was the sheriff.

"Help me," I said. "Mary's there."

I pointed to the wreckage of the helicopter and the truck, engulfed in flames, and I knew Mary was beyond help.

The sheriff called an ambulance for me and stayed with me until it came.

"The stick-up in McAllister was a diversion," he said. "I had a police artist from Helena draw sketches of the three men that killed Herbert Adams from Sam Culpepper's description of them, and I had a hunch and took them with me. They were I.D.'d as the robbers by the attendant. He pulled a gun and they shot him but he's going to live. They did the stick-up to draw me away from Virginia City and it worked. I'm sorry about Mary. Things might have been different if I had been here."

He looked down at the ground. I didn't respond. All I could think was that he was right, things might have been different if he was here, but he wasn't and now Mary was dead. I looked around at the activity taking place now that the shooting was over.

The volunteer fire department had arrived and was setting up to water down the two closest buildings to the hotel, The Opera House and the Railroad Depot, giving up on any effort to save the hotel. One whole side of the pedestrian street of Old Town was in shambles, the roofs and second floor balconies that had shaded the wood board sidewalk now in the street, in some cases pulling the second floors of the buildings down with them. The windows of the Sauerbier Blacksmith Shop were shot out and its front was chewed up by bullet holes, as was the board sidewalk in front of the Bale of Hay Saloon.

As I watched, the Green Front Hotel collapsed and the resulting cloud of sparks and embers was blown by the wind toward Old Town. The embers and firebrands flew past the Opera House and into the debris, and the fallen roofs and buildings were soon ablaze, beyond the reach of the hoses of the volunteer fire department. The sheriff rose and looked hopelessly at Old Town.

"Jesus," he said, "it looks like the burning of Atlanta in *Gone with the Wind*."

At last the ambulance arrived and I was taken to the hospital.

epilogue

    I followed the investigation in the morning papers while I was hospitalized. The sheriff announced that two of the men shot to death in the square had been positively identified as the murderers of Herbert Adams and involved in the McAllister robbery the morning of the fire. They were from Las Vegas and connected to Tony Danzante, alleged to be the head of a crime family and the owner of the Capri in Las Vegas, where he resided. There were three bodies in the helicopter, burned beyond recognition, but the sheriff believed that one was that of Danzante, who was crippled, one was that of the pilot and the third was that of the remaining man involved in the murder of Adams and the McAllister robbery. He speculated that the McAllister robbery had been a diversion to draw him away from Virginia City, where Danzante expected to recover from his ex-mistress, Theresa Defoe, a ledger she had taken from him which allegedly implicated him in income tax evasion and money laundering. She was killed during the shootout in Old Town when the helicopter crashed into a truck in which she was a passenger. Jeb Breckenridge, a local tow truck operator and the driver of the truck, was seen running from the crash and is wanted for the murder of Tom Faris, a retired L.A.P.D. officer living in Henry's Lake, Idaho, who was shot and killed at the scene, allegedly by Breckenridge. Faris and his former partner on the L.A.P.D., Mike Driscoll, were attempting to obtain evidence implicating Tony Danzante and other organized crime figures in income tax evasion and money laundering, and to arrest two of the men responsible for the murder of Herbert Adams, when the shooting erupted. Driscoll was wounded in the leg and is hospitalized.

The next day the papers were full of the Las Vegas link and agents from the FBI and Treasury Department came to interview me. When they heard about Mary's safe deposit box they got a court order to open it and they hit the jackpot. Not just the money and jewelry—Mary had made a photocopy of the ledger and rolled it up to fit in the box. I guess she was planning to ask Tony for more when the five million ran out. The Feds took the jewelry along with the money because I told them that Mary said she bought part of the jewelry with skim money. Nobody but Mary knew how much, so they kept it all.

The FAA showed up to investigate the crash of the helicopter and, after looking through the wreckage, they simply accepted my statement that the crash was caused by the pilot's being shot with a high-powered rifle and that ended the investigation. The metal of the chopper had melted in the fire and there was no way to tell where it came from. The car that Gino and Frankie parked at the entrance to Old Town was stolen in Las Vegas, and it was theorized that the helicopter also came from Las Vegas and was there to pick up Gino and

Frankie after they had shot us and had possession of the ledger. It was a day of double crosses.

Although the charred wreckage of the helicopter was

gone over carefully and the ashes around it were sifted, Tony's pinky ring with its huge diamond was never found, leading to speculation that it wasn't really Tony in the chopper. No one seemed to care that I had seen him fly right by me before the crash. Conspiracy theory always gets more ink than the facts, and so the legend of Tony was born.

Mary's parents came forward to claim what there was of her remains. The story of the burning of Old Town in Virginia City—coupled with crime, sex and Las Vegas—was big news, and pictures of Mary at her most beautiful had been splashed all over the media. Her parents recognized her from the photos although she had run away from her home in Austin, Minnesota, many years ago.

Mary's jewelry had been valued in the news stories at many millions of dollars and at first I thought they were ghouls trying to stake a claim to it and fight it out with the Feds, but then they showed me a picture of Mary in her high school annual, and even though the name under the picture was Matilda Costello, it was Mary, only younger. No wonder she changed her name. It was true, they were her parents.

Their names were Charles and Bridget Costello, and Charles had worked at the Hormel plant in Austin as a truck driver for over thirty years before he retired. I asked if Matilda was adopted and their only child, remembering what Mary had told me about her dysfunctional childhood when we were parked at the turnout for Old Faithful in Yellowstone, and they looked at each other and laughed for the first time. "Goodness no," Bridget said, "Matilda was the youngest of eight children, five boys and three girls."

I didn't give up, I had to know if any part of Mary's story was true, so I asked as delicately as possible, "Did you ask Matilda to leave when you found out she was pregnant?"

Bridget reacted angrily. "She never got pregnant. Where did you hear an awful story like that?"

"From Mary, I mean Matilda," I replied.

The father broke in. "After she graduated from high school, I got her a job at the Hormel plant packing pickled pigs' feet in glass jars. It was a good job and paid well, but Matilda hated it. She ran away with the foreman after she had been on the job for about three months and that's the last we ever saw of her. The foreman had a wife and three kids and he showed up six months later. He said Matilda had dumped him in New York. We hired private detectives and did everything we could to find her, but we never heard from her or anything about her until the pictures of her in the papers.

"Austin is a small town and the foreman leaving his wife and kids for Matilda was a big scandal. At lot of people at church stopped speaking to us because of it and I was told by the company that I should retire since I had thirty years in and all but I knew the reason was Matilda. One of our daughters was pretty serious with a boy at the time and his parents made him break up with her. It was a big tragedy for us in more ways than one but we still worried about her and wanted to know if she was all right, and we would have taken her back in a minute if she showed up at our door regardless of what the people in town thought of her or of us. To hell with them."

His voice trailed off. "But we never saw her again."

Bridget put her arm around his shoulders.

It didn't sound like Mary would be welcome in Austin, or want to go back there, and I said so. They nodded sadly and then I told them that Mary and I were going to be married and live in Virginia City and, with their permission, I would like to bury her here where she would be happy. After all, that's what she told me. What's not to believe?

They said they would like that and after I got out of the hospital we buried her in the little cemetery in Virginia City. Not many people came to the funeral, Bob and Thelma Hill and some of the gang from Curly's, but Sam Culpepper gave a nice eulogy and her folks said they felt better knowing she was with people who loved her. Before they left town they turned over to Virginia City whatever claim they had to Mary's jewelry as a gift for the rebuilding of Old Town, and now the Feds will have a fight on their hands. The Costellos were nice people.

I buried Mary in a duplex plot. That means that when I die I'll be buried on top of her and I liked the idea since we spent so much time in that position. She had tried to double cross me, so what? She loved me more than anything except money and that was good enough for me.

Jeb Breckenridge was picked up in Mary's car in Butte after he got into a fight in a bar. He said that everything was Mary's idea and her car had been left at Sam's garage for them to make a getaway after they held us up for the five million dollars. He was pretty confused and didn't understand how he had gotten into so much trouble so fast and I almost felt sorry for him. Almost, but not quite.

Bob Hill told me that his deputy on vacation in Hawaii had called to say he was not coming back and never wanted to see snow again and the job was mine if I wanted it. I told him I would be proud to work for him and he swore me in right there. He still had an opening to fill and he said that he had thought a lot about what Mary had said and asked what I thought about hiring a woman deputy. I thanked him and said it would be a great tribute to Mary.

Sam Culpepper sold the garage and bought a tour bus to serve the people drawn to Virginia City to see the site of the shoot-out at the Green Front Hotel, as it became known, and the remains of Old Town. Even in the dead of winter the motels were packed with tourists and the Chamber of Commerce predicted that next summer would be the biggest ever for business in Virginia City. There was talk of building a set of Old Town, like in the movies, and burning it down every year. What a tourist attraction that would be!

Sam stops the bus in front of the sheriff's office a couple of times a day and asks me to come outside so his passengers can see me.

"Yes-sirree," he announces, "I told you folks about the sheriff who got himself hung way back in 1864, but here's a real live sheriff that was in the shoot-out at the Green Front Hotel and that's going to be our next stop."

I've got to tell him to cut it out, but he's such a nice old guy that I just can't do it.

I go to Curly's for dinner a lot but I'm no longer the Bull Moose. I finally got to Helena for that A.A. meeting and now I'm off of everything so I order sarsaparilla at the bar. Everyone's nice and friendly but they just can't handle their Bull Moose drinking sarsaparilla.

I'm living in the little house, still without a picket fence, renting from the estate of Herbert Adams. I got rid of the bed because of him, partly because his blood was all over it but mostly because he was all over Mary in it. The estate is trying to peddle the house but without much luck because of the murder of Herbert in it and I will probably make a bid on it one of these days. I would like to get a bargain at Herbert's expense. It seems to me he owes me one.

Bob and Thelma Hill have invited me to dinner a couple of times and there's always a single woman they want to introduce to me. I guess that means I'm an eligible bachelor again and the casserole brigade has started. Even Harriet Smith from across the street stopped over all gussied up and carrying a tuna casserole that she said had been in the family for ages. It certainly tasted like it.

I go out to the cemetery to see Mary and bring flowers and talk to her. Once I called her Matilda Costello to let her know that I knew her real name and then I said it was nice to know that I could count on her being in Virginia City with me for a long time. It had been threatening to rain all day and right then there was a flash of lightning and a clap of thunder. I think she was trying to tell me something but maybe I'm superstitious. I was going to tell her that the money in the bag was mostly cut paper but I changed my mind after the thunder and lightning.

I think a lot about Sally and the date we had at Canaletto and how I messed it up. If I had kissed her maybe I wouldn't have gone back to Virginia City except to get my car and Mary would be alive today. I also want to test my theory that I can win in Vegas every time it rains, so maybe I'll go down there when I get some time off and the weather is right and see what happens.